POUGH
KEEPSIE
SHUFFLE

DIETRICH KALTEIS
POUGH KEEPSIE SHUFFLE

ECW PRESS
TORONTO

Published by ECW Press
665 Gerrard Street East
Toronto, Ontario, Canada M4M 1Y2
416-694-3348 / info@ecwpress.com

Cover design: David A. Gee
Typesetting: Erika Head
Author photo: © Andrea Kalteis

LIBRARY AND ARCHIVES CANADA
CATALOGUING IN PUBLICATION

Kalteis, Dietrich, author
Poughkeepsie shuffle / Dietrich Kalteis.

Issued in print and electronic formats.

ISBN 978-1-77041-401-3 (softcover)
ALSO ISSUED AS: 978-1-77305-247-2 (EPUB),
978-1-77305-248-9 (PDF)

I. Title.

PS8621.A474P68 2018   C813'.6
C2018-902545-X   C2018-902546-8

The publication of *Poughkeepsie Shuffle* has been generously supported by the Canada Council
for the Arts, which last year invested $153 million to bring the arts to Canadians throughout
the country. *Nous remercions le Conseil des arts du Canada de son soutien. L'an dernier, le Conseil a
investi 153 millions de dollars pour mettre de l'art dans la vie des Canadiennes et des Canadiens de tout
le pays.* We also acknowledge the support of the Ontario Arts Council (OAC), an agency of the
Government of Ontario, which last year funded 1,737 individual artists and 1,095 organizations in
223 communities across Ontario for a total of $52.1 million, and the contribution of the Government
of Ontario through the Ontario Book Publishing Tax Credit and the Ontario Media Development
Corporation.

PRINTED AND BOUND IN CANADA   PRINTING: WEBCOM   5   4   3   2   1

REMEMBERING PAISLEY
AN EXTRAORDINARY FRIEND

...GIVING THE FINGER

Robbie Boyd stepped from the showroom doors, locking up Bracey's AutoPark, catching the stockyard air coming from a block away. Feeling as rumpled as his suit, Robbie ran a hand through his thinning hair, looking to the street. Going to the *Toronto Sun* box at the curb, he dropped in a quarter and took a look at the front page. The Big Board doing a nosedive, the Jays winning one at home, and a couple of gangbangers gunned down in another Rexdale drive-by, the northwest of the city turning into a war zone. Flipping the page, Robbie gave the sunshine girl a seven and rolled up the paper.

Starting work at nine in the a.m., he'd sold a Monte Carlo to the first guy through the door, some hick who drove down from Stouffville, believed every word Robbie told him about the turbo model with the strato buckets and the previous owner who only put ten thousand true klicks on the odometer. The rest of day, Robbie drank too much Nescafé and passed cards and smiles to a bunch of tire kickers, pretty sure two would come back. Minus the pack, he'd clear nearly enough on the Monte Carlo to meet next month's rent.

The Canuck buck was making a slow crawl from the toilet, and Ted Bracey, the guy who owned the AutoPark, was buying cars at auctions in upstate New York, detailing them and sending them north. Promised to raise the sliding scale if the buck crept higher. Ted had hired an ex-con named Vick DuMont, fresh out of the Don, and mentioned over lunch at the deli he was thinking about appointing Robbie to sales manager.

Long on promises, Ted Bracey had been paying Robbie the mini since the place opened. Robbie living on those promises and skinny commissions since the spring.

Looking in the direction of Gunns Loop, Robbie mulled jumping on the one-eyed streetcar, betting it would be packed armpit to armpit. Better to just walk the dozen blocks to home, stop for a cold one at Captain Jack's, two bucks for a pint of Molson's till seven. Twice in the last week, some afterwork babes had drifted in for the happy hour, and one of them, tall with thick-framed glasses, had been looking down the bar, glancing Robbie's way. But Robbie would end up alone, nuking himself a Stouffer's and thumbing the remote, nodding off to Johnny and Ed, same as always. But still, it was something, maybe it was hope.

The old Booker Jones number was rolling through his head again, been stuck there all day. The one about being down since he began to crawl. A grey Ford Econoline pulled to the curb just before he got to Old Weston, exhaust note like a cry for help, a Maltese cross dangling from its rearview. Twenty years since the heap rolled off some Detroit assembly line. One of the double doors on the side creaked open. A guy with a thick neck and dirty, blond hair squatted inside, a bent Rand McNally in his hand, giving the smile of the lost tourist. The guy behind the wheel turned his head and smiled, too.

"Where you boys want to be?" Robbie said, taking them for out-of-towners in for the Jays game, second in the series.

"Got messed around." Flapping open the map book, the blond guy said, "Man, this city's something, huh? Nothing runs the way you think."

"Ought to try the Gardiner after a doubleheader, same time as the Ex. Want to talk about gridlock." Cocking his head, Robbie tried making sense of the guy's map, asking again where they wanted to be.

Climbing out, the driver came around the back, hands in his pockets, leaning in close like he wanted to see the map, nudging something into Robbie's ribs, something sharp.

The blond guy saying, "Get in."

"Hey, easy, come on . . . got hardly any cash on me." Robbie dropped the book, looking around for help, the guy inside catching his wrist. The one behind him shoving, kicking the paper under the van.

The blond guy hit Robbie in the gut. The driver slammed the door, looking casual as he went around back and got behind the wheel, working the Ford-O-Matic, coaxing the eighty-five horses to life.

Rolling his tongue around his mouth, Robbie checked for teeth, struggling to say, "You got the wrong —"

Blond guy swung the fist, putting Robbie flat, saying, "Man talks when he should be listening, huh, Egg?"

Grunting about not calling him by name, Egg kept his eyes on the road, dealing with the traffic, crossing Dufferin.

Pulling out a roll of strapping tape, blond guy said nicknames meant shit and swung a leg across Robbie, zipping off about a foot and clapping it over his mouth. "Fact, I go by Bundy. Never gonna say it to nobody, I right, Robbie?" His knees pressed into Robbie's shoulders.

Robbie nodded his head.

"Good boy." Patting Robbie down, Bundy took the wallet from the windbreaker pocket, checking his ID, the new photo license, holding the likeness close to Robbie's face. "Yeah, we got the right guy."

Robbie thinking maybe he sold these guys a lemon one time. Maybe the one he was lying in. Robbie finding it hard to breathe just through his nose. Unable to talk through the tape, his lips stuck together, pressing at the tape with his tongue.

"Do me a favor, think you can do that, Robbie?" Bundy asked.

Robbie gave another nod, like sure, sure.

"Want you to pass on a message. Think you can do that?"

Robbie kept nodding.

"Tell your boss, here's what happens when you don't pay what you owe. You with me?"

Robbie stopped nodding, looking doubtful.

Pulling a pair of garden pruners from a pocket, Bundy flipped off the safety catch and snapped its parrot jaws, saying, "You tell that son of a bitch, he's got till end of next week. Next finger's gonna be his. You got it?"

Fuck!

The scream into the tape came out like a long moan, Robbie trying to buck Bundy off.

Landing a slap, Bundy told him to hold the fuck still. "These things are fuckin' sharp."

Robbie couldn't breathe, panicking, trying to jerk his hand away from the blades.

Locking hold of the wrist, Bundy said, "How about a tune there, Egg?"

Lifting a boom box off the passenger floor, Egg faced it to the back and wedged it between the buckets. Egg twisted the volume knob and pressed play. "Addicted to Love" pumped through the speakers, Egg driving on, tapping his fat fingers on the wheel.

Robbie bucked and writhed, Bundy forcing his finger between the jaws.

Snip.

"There we go, nothing to it." Bundy rode the convulsing Robbie, the man's eyes bugging. Holding up the digit, Bundy showed it to him, saying except for the fingernail, it looked like one of the sausage links he'd downed for breakfast.

Fighting the spin down the black hole, Robbie kept from passing out. Egg turned right past the old Joy Oil station, checked his mirrors, stopped on the side street and switched off the boom box. Reaching a tub of Wet-Naps, he passed them back.

Propping Robbie up, Bundy pulled a few tissues, clapping the man on the back like he'd been a good sport, warning him about going to the cops. He took a couple more tissues and wrapped the pinkie, handing it to Robbie. "There's a clinic a couple doors up. Hurry, maybe they can, you know, reattach it." Bundy pointed past the station. Yanking the handle, he pushed the side door open with a foot, zipping the tape from Robbie's mouth, helping him out, Bundy saying, "Watch your step there, and Robbie . . ."

Robbie turned, clamping his jaws, the pain sharp and shooting through him.

"Remember the part about no cops, huh? Coulda been worse, huh? Coulda been your pecker. Just so we understand each other."

Nodding, tears starting. Clutching the injured hand with the other, Robbie didn't take a step until the Econoline turned on St. Clair and pulled away. He stumbled past the station, dripping blood down his sleeve. In shock. The pain becoming more intense.

It was a vet clinic called Paws 'N Claws. Robbie stood there rapping with his elbow, then he kicked at the wood door a couple of times, yelling, looking in the window for anybody moving around inside. He couldn't get himself to look down at the hand and the wrapped finger.

. . . BETWEEN JOBS

"Okay, so you met this guy, getting your hair cut?" Ann Hibbit looked at me like she was waiting for the punch line.

"Yeah, guy from back in the day."

"By back in the day, you mean the Don Jail?"

"Got to start, huh?" Prying my fingernail at the cigarette burn on the Formica table, the yellow moonglow pattern from the sixties. "Anyway, this guy Vick's sitting in the next chair, towel around his neck, getting some off the top." No point telling her Marcel's barbershop was a front for ex-cons looking for the kind of work nobody posted in the want ads. Marcel Banks, former alumnus of the Don himself, was the guy you went to see once you got released, putting guys like me into the kind of jobs that didn't show on any company books. Collections and strong-arm stuff mostly, somebody in need of a wheel man, some muscle or protection, skill sets you didn't find at Manpower.

"Just don't tell me it's commission," Ann said, looking at me over her shoulder.

"All the time ragging about me finding work, now you got to get picky."

"Come on, Jeff, commission, you can't count on that. My granddad did it after the war, barely scraped by —"

"Different times. Top of that, the last guy, guy named Robbie, just walked out and didn't give notice. This guy Bracey, owner of the place, needs somebody pronto. See, Vick tells me the outfit imports cars from the States, leaving fat margins and bigger commission than your average car lot. You ask me, I call that a break." I didn't tell her the part about Ted Bracey smuggling guns under the chassis of the cars coming north, the AutoPark making a perfect front. Marcel Banks lining me up just like he did Vick. Liked that I knew my way around cars, giving me points for never ratting out the outfit I stole for.

"Come on, what do you know about selling cars? You got sent up for stealing them. Like that qualifies."

"Funny girl," I said. She used to be fun before I got sentenced. That smile and bright eyes that first hooked me. Still, Ann had hung in and waited while I served the better part of the deuce after setting my Jose Cuervo on the roof of this late-model Buick I was jacking from a car lot in Malton, middle of nowhere. Sliding my slim jim between the door and window, I popped the lock, got in and crossed the wires. Just my dumb luck, a two-man security patrol rolled by as I pulled off the lot, the bottle sliding off the roof. Didn't even bother trying to outrun them.

Aside from waiting, Ann wrote the letter about true devotion, part of the plan I submitted to the parole board, them seeing her as my support network upon my release back into the community.

"So your con buddy gets you this job . . ."

"Ex-con."

"Great, an ex-con. Thought you had to stay clear of guys like that."

"The man's reformed, same as me," I said.

Vick DuMont did time for his part in a film tank turned fish farm, place called TrueNorth up in Uxbridge. The former catering to the film industry coming north for the cheap Canuck buck, the latter serving a handful of second-rate eateries. Vick told me all that on the ride from the courthouse to the Don, how things might have worked out if the rainbow trout hadn't caught this fucking virus, most of them going belly up in a single night. The Board of Health inspectors coming in stumbled upon some falsified operating expenses, leading to financial restatements and unexplained company funds in Vick's personal account. The health guys tipped the fed auditors, who discovered he'd been suspected by the OPP of arson in a cardboard furniture scam a year before. Instead of landing the insurance claim on the fish, Vick got a three-year stretch.

"How about I get past the interview," I said, "maybe get offered the job, then you chew me out. How'd that be, huh?"

She went quiet, stirring chips into cookie dough, Ann liking the place filled with that nice cookie aroma. Said it made the place feel homey, like when she was growing up. Eggs, butter and packets cluttered the counter. A flour handprint streaked her cheek. She puffed at wisps of hair. A couple of times now, she'd talked about raising kids, never asking how I felt about it. The box of pregnancy strips in the drawer next to the Pill dispenser on her side of the bed made me uneasy. Every morning after we got vertical, the woman went in the can, had me guessing she was peeing on the litmus.

Working the spigot of the box of burgundy on the corner of the table — three liters for the price of two — I splashed the juice glass full. The wine going down easy.

Plopping lumps of dough on the parchment, Ann shoved the tin sheet in the oven, sipping from her own glass.

"Know nobody's jumping to hire ex-cons, right?" I said, a chip of Formica coming loose under my nail. Flicking it across the kitchen, I remembered that feeling of me and Vick being led up the steps into the Don, glancing up at that mawkish stone carving of Father Time looking down over the entrance to that hellhole. Gargoyles on the cat-walks added to the creepy feel of the place. The prick guard who led us in pointed out the rotunda where they used to flog the inmates. The guard's name was Ruby, and he told us about some inmate performing a swan dive from the top balcony just a week back, the guy was weak and just couldn't take it anymore. Making a detour, Ruby showed us the skinny cells in the old wing, how the inmates used to get a bucket for a toilet, the scratches in the plaster where they counted off their days. The old death row with its own gallows room, that section shut down back in seventy-seven, Ruby wanting us to know it was there, giving us something to think about. Saying guys like us coming in these days had it soft, told us to make ourselves at home.

"Don't do that," Ann said, slapping my hand away from the chip in the Formica. "Isn't it bad enough?" She looked at the crap table she'd hauled home from out back of the Salvation Army store. Came upon it on her way to visitation, coming to see me just that one time, picking up the dangling phone and looking at me through the glass. She told me how she wedged it in the trunk of my old Valiant, tying the lid down with a rope and a bungee, having to haul it home on her own, gave her a sore back for a week.

Pushing back my chair, I stepped up behind her and worked my hands into the muscles of her shoulders, not wanting to fight. It took a moment, but she got into it and swayed like there was music, liking what I was doing. Always said I was good with my hands. She'd packed on a few pounds, not that it bothered me — this woman baking cookies all the time, having to eat them on her own for the last eighteen months.

I told her this job was about more than selling cars. Bracey's AutoPark in the Junction buying pre-owns at auction, shipping them up from New York State, getting them detailed at their shop in Poughkeepsie, Bracey taking advantage of the exchange rates.

"Meaning?"

"Meaning it leaves more margin, see?"

"Maybe," she said. Then she told me about this place she'd seen for sale, a fix-me-upper over by Baby Point, place with blue shutters. Saw the feature sheet pasted in the window of the Re/Max office over by the strip mall.

I listened to her tell about it, smiling and saying, "Yeah, maybe down the road."

Sighing, she pulled away and went about snugging elastics around sacks of sugar and flour, putting them in the cupboard. Looking at me, saying she wasn't getting any younger, then she said, "Oh, and Deb called, says to say hello."

"Great."

"Her birthday last week."

"Yeah, forty again?"

"Funny man. Oh, speaking of cars, Dennis surprised her with new wheels. Parked it in the driveway with a big bow on it. Gonna send me a picture."

Guess she needed to take a poke, waiting eighteen months while her clock was ticking. Ann having to rip the cord on the old Toro, dealing with the looks from the neighbors who somehow found out I was doing time. Her sister, Deb Ryan, offering to put a dish on the roof of our rental dump, send money for pay-TV, let Ann tune in the *20 Minute Workout* and get Superchannel while she waited for me to get my release. I hated the thought of taking hand-outs, especially from her sister.

"Dennis just wants her in something safe," she said.

"Uh huh, what's safe?"

"Red Beemer, the little cute one, you know . . ."

"Uh huh." Stole one once, an old 2002, not a bad ride. Shoving my glass under the spigot, I worked it with my thumb, refilling the glass, feeling the wine now, leaning back in the chair, saying, "Dennis getting into grand theft auto now, huh?"

"Takes one to know one," she said, then, "Anyway, I'm happy for her, she deserves it."

I should have left it alone, but I said, "The guy hawks chemical fertilizer, and Deb runs a tacky knickknack in a strip mall. How much can they make?"

"Well, enough for a red Beemer."

I shook my head, grinning. "Nothing worse than new money."

"No money." She grinned back.

Waving a finger at her, I said, "Don't go using your mother's face on me, okay?"

Splashing wine in her own glass, she said she was sorry she mentioned it, but didn't look it. Catching her hand, I swung her into my lap, careful not to spill any wine, saying, "You're a true ball buster, you know it?"

"Yeah, I know it." She kissed me, saying, "Red Beemer's gonna look good in front of their new place." Smirking and grinding her hips in my lap, saying, "Oh, and Dennis booked them on a cruise, the two of them going to Alaska." Arcing her back, she let me get my hand under her top.

"One of them polluters of the seas, huh?" I said, sliding my hand around her back, under the strap, trying to work those two bastard hooks. "What's next, a pair of side-by-side plots, some fancy-ass cemetery?"

Ann laughed, pushing my hand away. Getting up, doing her herself back up.

"Least what we got's ours," I said, reaching my glass.

"Right." She took the tray from the oven, the cookies nice and brown, setting them on the stovetop. Then she picked up the wooden spoon like a microphone and spoke to it, "Oh, was that the door?" Turning her head, she waited till I looked down the hall, saying, "Why, it's Robin Leach. Oh, do come in, Robin. Yes, allow our houseman to take your coat, and oh, a tour, sure . . . why, where do we start?"

I refilled my glass, shaking my head and watching her.

Ann talking to the spoon. "Yes, let's film the leaky garage first, shall we?" Making a Vanna White hand gesture. "Why yes, that's our import parked in its own juices. Just fabulous, isn't it? A Valiant, yes, from the Stone Age, all bought and paid for."

Had me shaking my head, Ann looking around, saying, "And yes, Robin, that is a real fireplace, but we don't use it much, not since it blew soot all over our priceless antiques. The two of us living in the lack of luxury, don't you know."

Picking at the Formica again, I was laughing and looking at her, feeling the wine, saying, "Yeah, well, least what we got, we own."

"Oh, God, Jesus, they're gonna laugh when they get a load of this place." She looked around and refilled her glass, stopped herself, and poured her glass into mine.

I looked at her, getting that sinking feeling, saying, "When who sees this place?"

She rolled her eyes, saying, "Stopping in on their way back to Montreal."

"Deb? Dennis?"

"Hmm hmm."

"And I'm hearing about it now?" I kicked at the table leg.

"It's just for a couple of days, Jeff." She went back to slapping more golf ball lumps of dough on another sheet. Ann not caring what they looked like now.

"That woman . . ." I shook my head, thinking of her sister here for a few days.

"She's blood . . . and Mother's getting on . . ."

"Mother? Oh, for fuck's . . ." Felt the current shoot through me, my foot kicking out again, the box of wine nearly tumbling. I jumped up and caught it.

"You know, I had friends before you came along, mister. Now nobody even calls anymore, and all I got's family . . . such as it is." Tossing the scoop in the sink, she glared at me. "Think you should see somebody, some kind of doctor, you know, maybe get a script."

"Naw, maybe I shouldn't see somebody — like Debra, Mother and . . ." I slapped a hand to my forehead.

"Spread the love, Jeff." Folding her arms in that way she had. The wall phone rang and she jumped, then reached for it, saying, "Hello?"

I heard the telemarketer speak his lines. "Hello, ma'am. How are we this fine evening?"

"Let me guess, you're going to tell me you got just what I need, right?" Pulling the cord tight, she came over and slapped my fingers from the chipped Formica again.

"If there's a better time for me to call, ma'am?" the tinny voice said.

"It just gets worse," Ann said, telling him to hold on, letting the receiver dangle to the floor. Taking the batch of cookies from the tray, she piled them into a tin that read *Home Sweet Home*. Pressing on the lid, she stomped from the room.

I watched the phone cord coil around the receiver, reminded me of a snake.

The tinny voice repeating hello.

Followed by dial tone.

Drinking the wine, I went back to thinking of the Don,

the grey-and-blue cubicles where they did the search-and-process. Took my personal belongings and shoved them in the blue bag, putting the numbered tag on it. Handing me the orange jumpsuit. I remembered that first whiff of morning scent. The sight of the hands hanging out between the blue cell bars. Books and bibles stuck between the bars like they were shelves. Guys giving each other the stink eye. That fucker Ruby grinning as he told me not to flush the lidless head at night on account of the noise. Thinking about the groups: the blacks in what they called Motown, the young offenders in Kiddy Corner, the long-timers in Pen Range. The high walls of the exercise yard that kept anybody on the outside from pitching anything to the guys in the yard. No doubt the place was hell. Drinking my wine, I compared it to doing time with Deb, Dennis and Mother. Couldn't decide which was worse.

. . . MAKING IT RIGHT

The girl the escort service sent over was Sinn-amon, looking up at him, not believing this old guy was reaching for the phone again. Second time he'd done it. Kneeling in front of him, leaning back and folding her arms.

Ted Bracey spoke into the phone, "Hey, Robbie, sorry my man, must've got disconnected. You were saying . . ."

"Fuck you, I quit."

"Come on, Robbie, you and me, we got history, my man. Can't just walk out. Say what it is, and I set it right."

"Fuckers did it with garden snips. Any idea of the pain?"

"Said I'm sorry, Robbie. Bet it's a bitch, no doubt, but, hey, you think I can call you back? Right in the middle of something."

Sinn-amon looked at him in his La-Z-Boy. Couldn't believe this guy. Whoever was on the line was screaming about paying what he owed.

"Said I'll make it right," Ted said, holding the phone away from his ear, telling her he'd only be a sec.

"How you gonna make it right?" Robbie said, the phone booth up the block from Toronto Western. "Fuckers dropped me in front of a vet. Fucking place was closed. Had to wave down a cab and get over here. Bleeding all over the guy's seat the whole way. Could've died, and the fucker charges me five bucks for a bullshit cleaning fee."

"What'd you tell them, the medics?"

"Said I got careless trimming my prize zinnias, the nurse writing on the chart thought I'd been drinking."

"Good man. You did right." Mal Rocca had sicced his dogs on Ted, the old shylock warning him about missing payments. Going after his guys now, sending his message. Ted smiled at the girl — forgot the name she was using — mouthed again he'd just be one more sec.

"I'm fucking disfigured, Ted," Robbie said, "holding up my hand, looking at the space where my finger should be. Goddamned popping pain killers like Tic Tacs."

"Which one they get?" Ted said.

"What?"

"Finger, which one?"

"Fuck's it matter?" Robbie was yelling again. "Finger's a finger."

"Like I said, Robbie, I'll make it right." Ted winking at the girl. Mouthing, "Big tip."

"How you gonna do that, Ted?"

"For starters, we get you protection . . ."

"What, gloves, mitts?"

"A gun, Robbie. Get you packing like a man. Somebody pulls shit on you —"

"I sell used fucking cars, do your books, for that I need a gun?"

"Looks like, yeah, plus you need your fingers for counting, right?"

"I'm holding one up now, a finger, Ted, you wanna guess which —"

Grabbing the phone from Ted, Sinn-amon hung it up, saying, "I know you paid me, mister, but you want this or not, 'cause if you don't . . ."

"Sorry, baby." Ted rested his hands on her head, ran his fingers through her hair, pulled her close and leaned back in the La-Z-Boy. Next time he called the escort service, he'd ask for his usual, Ginger, the one they'd been sending over for the last year. That girl understood him. He figured she must be on vacation.

●

Dial tone. Robbie looked at the phone. Reaching his good hand in a pocket, he took the pill bottle, popped the lid with his thumb and downed a couple more Percodan. Didn't matter about the side effects or what it said on the label. Stepping to the curb, he waved his bandaged hand at another yellow cab. Robbie needed that drink, looking at his watch, happy hour at Captain Jack's was long over.

. . . COULD BE BIG

Taking the last plate from the dishwasher, Ann checked it for chips and toweled it dry, doing what the old machine couldn't, the landlord refusing to upgrade the defunct Norge, saying they didn't make them like that anymore. Closing the cupboard door, she hung the towel on the knob. Sitting across from me, she flicked my hand from the chipped Formica again, saying she knew I could do better.

"What's better?"

"A real job, you know, a place where you go, nine to five, five days a week, get a paycheck."

"Haven't even met with the man, and you're at me."

"How we supposed to get by on what I make? Don't want me borrowing from Deb or Mother, right?"

"Look, Vick's been doing alright. Only been there a month or so, and he's making decent sales . . ."

"Since he got out?"

I was wishing I never told her how we met, the transfer from the court building to Broadview and Gerrard. The two of us talking in back of the wagon on the way to the east wing. Both of us looking up at old Father Time in front of the Don as we were led inside.

"Nobody's saying you got to put Don Jail on your résumé, Jeff. Maybe bend the truth a bit. Nobody checks."

Sitting in the two barber chairs that day at Marcel's the day I got released, Vick looked at me, popped his eyebrows the way he did, and said, "Holy shit, brother, they let you out, huh?" Offering his hand.

Taking a little off the top, Marcel laid it out for me. Ted Bracey ran the AutoPark, a front for running guns up from the States. The man was in need of a couple guys posing as car salesmen, the last guy not working out. Since Vick got onboard, Ted was playing it cautious, not saying much about the smuggling yet, feeling Vick out.

According to Marcel, the cars had cells welded under the chassis, the cells packed with guns. Others had pistols in vacuum-sealed bags hidden in the gas tanks. Bracey was looking for another guy like Vick who could stand some heat, sell some cars while they were at it.

"Can't afford any more of your pipe dreams and short-cuts," Ann said.

"We got to do this dance, Ann? Look, you're worried, I get that, really. You want, we take in another homestay, at least till I get this on track."

"Easy for you, sitting in your cell. I'll never forget walking in on that last kid pulling his . . . aww . . ." Ann cringed, the last homestay student didn't last a week. Ann still seeing the kid's belly shake as he pumped his fist, sitting on the bed. The sheets she'd just picked up at Honest Ed's.

"Okay, so that was one time."

"More than plenty, believe me. Seeing something like that . . . just be glad I still . . ." She waved it off, saying, "And where you suppose it . . . uh, God, my baby's not crawling through that."

There it was again, Ann having thoughts of a baby. The woman's clock was ticking like a bomb, louder as she closed in on forty. Barely back in the world, I was trying to put my life together. In a year, I'd be hitting fifty, sure wasn't the time for drooling dependents. Could barely take care of myself. Picking up the glass, I swallowed some more wine, saying, "Just gonna talk to this guy, hear him out. That's it." Saying it louder, like it was final.

Marcel had said Ted Bracey was in tight with the Bent Boys up in Rexdale, the gang in the middle of a turf war with the Dreads. Ready and willing to pay cash for all the firepower Bracey could get. Marcel saying there was money to be made. Big money.

Sitting on his deck with the cedar hedge at his back, Vick DuMont tapped his fingers on the arm of the metal chair. He tried for cool, not letting his eyes go to the portable drill on the picnic table.

Randy Hooper stood close, letting his size get his point across, his hair hanging in front of his face, strands sticking together like he'd been sweating. Pony White leaned against the shakes of the post-war-era house and looked on. Frown lines deep as scars on either side of his mouth.

Randy saying, "Two ways we can go." Sitting on the bench of the picnic table, leaning close to Vick, Randy reached in a pocket and took a banded roll of cash, holding it up. Looked like a grand in hundreds. Tossing it, he caught it, saying to Pony, "Why they got to go the hard way all the time?"

"Beats me."

Setting the cash on the table, Randy picked up the drill, *Boar Gun* printed on the side, big battery pack on the bottom. Pressing the trigger, he spun the bit, looked like he admired it, saying, "One way's money, Vick, other way's pain."

"Okay, said I'll find out what I can."

"Expect your call, then," Randy said, spinning the bit and gouging into the top of the table, saying, "You do, you get another roll like this one. You don't . . ." He drilled deeper.

"Said I would, right?" Vick wiped at his forehead. Looking at the hole, he threw in that Ted Bracey had a trailer load of cars coming across the Peace Bridge, told them about the hidden cells welded underneath, opened on hydraulics. How you had to tap your foot on the brake and turn the key at the same time, flip a switch under a fake bottom on the console for the cells to open. Each packed with a couple of Uzis.

"Already know all that, the reason we're talking. What I want to know's when and where," Randy said, tapping the drill bit against the roll of cash, then tapping it against the side of Vick's knee. "Whichever one you want, your choice."

"All I know, swear," Vick said.

"But you'll find out more," Randy tapped the trigger, let the bit spin, catching the edge of Vick's pants.

"Yeah, yeah." Eyes on the bit, Vick bobbed his head and moved his leg away.

Randy got up, taking the drill, going and opening the screen. Vick's schnauzer rushed out, Randy giving it a pat, then walking through the house, boots thudding on the hardwood.

Standing there, looking at the roll of bills, Pony said, "We got this place, kind of a warehouse sitting empty, out by the nuke plant. Locals moved the fuck away after the bullshit over in Chernobyl. You hear about it?"

"Yeah, yeah, sure." Vick nodded.

"Nobody wants a CANDU reactor in the hood. Place getting all deserted." Pony pointed at the gouge in the table. "We got to start drilling more holes, nobody's gonna hear the screaming, not out there. You get me?" Pony left him sitting there, going through the house. Vick on the metal chair, hugging his dog.

. . . BOUNCE

Checking the paperwork, the DOT number, the Canada Customs inspector looked at the bill of lading and manifest. Bucky Showalter watched him do the secondary, walking axle to axle with the mirror on the stick, checking under the Peterbilt. Eyeballing the half dozen cars chained up the trailer, all American and full-sized: the Gran Fury, a Granada, a 98, a T-Bird and a couple of Crown Vics. Sitting easy behind the wheel, he peeled off his shades, rubbing the miles from his eyelids. Waiting.

The Lewiston crossing wasn't normally busy this time of day. Bucky watching the advance lights, the inspector finally waving him on. Bucky making a grand on this haul, double what he got for crossing state lines.

Back when he made the first run for Mateo Cruz from Poughkeepsie to Toronto, Bucky knew he was hauling more than just the cars. When he said he'd do this run, he guessed Mateo had his guys pack the cars with coke or pot, something they'd want north of the border. None of his business and nothing he wanted to know about. If the inspector found anything, that dumb look of surprise was going to help get him off. Just the driver, Bucky was scraping a living, had mouths to feed back on a dot on a map, place called Fishkill.

Parking where the guy in the uniform pointed, Bucky let her idle and stepped down. He went and paid the toll, then went to the pay phone outside. Fishing a quarter, he punched in a number, waiting, hearing the click, the operator asking someone at the other end about accepting the charges. Bucky waited for Ted Bracey's voice, saying, "Yeah man, it's me, just passed through." Listened, then said, "Uh huh, be there in a bit, just gonna stop for a quick bite first." Then he hung up. Walking easy back to the cab, he flicked a salute to the guy in the booth. Yuh, an easy grand.

●

Behind his desk, Ted Bracey set the phone down, turning the volume back up on the Sony on the bureau, CFTO running the news, Tom Gibney looking serious, talking about the mounting gang war in the city.

"Haven't seen nothing yet," Ted said.

Gibney talking about illegal firearms making their way into the country, the RCMP investigating. Ted smiled, thinking Bucky Showalter just crossed at Lewiston. No problem slipping right in. Ted's man Mateo Cruz taking care of welding on the cells at the Poughkeepsie shop, Mateo swearing the Uzis couldn't be detected.

Gibney was reporting how authorities found a couple of Uzis at the scene, footage running of the aftermath of the latest bloodbath: three bodies face down on the pavement, cars shot up, windows of a local grocery blown out. Gibney saying police were trying to trace the source of the weapons.

"Fresh from the Six-Day War," Ted told him. "Nine-millimeter with the thirty-two extended magazines, twin-folding metal strut stocks and black poly grips." He pointed at the screen, an officer being interviewed, holding one of the weapons, saying it could fire a couple hundred rounds a minute. "Try six hundred rounds," Ted said. "Baby weighs just three and a half pounds, easy to tuck inside of cars. Fetches two grand a pop."

The screen switched back to Gibney in the studio, saying several handguns were also found at the scene.

Ted nodding, saying to the TV, "Mateo's crew uses an old Dazey Seal-a-Meal machine. Vacuum seals bags of pistols right in the gas tanks."

Gibney telling how police suspected a Rexdale gang, the Bent Boys.

"And those boys just drooling for more guns, paying me half up front." Ted thinking he'd make enough from this run to get Mal Rocca, the fucking loan shark, off his back. Money Ted had needed to open this dealership.

Gibney went on, the Bents waging war with the More-land Dreads, killing each other over drug turf. More footage running across the screen: four more gang members gunned down over this past week, a drive-by with no arrests. Gibney stacking the count at nine in the past two months.

"As long as they pay cash, it's all good." Ted watched, the screen showing Dustin, the eldest Bent, after he'd been gunned down two weeks back in Steeltown.

"Partied the night away," Ted said. "Should've looked before stepping from the Regent."

Gibney saying an unnamed woman and the valet were also caught in the open, a muscle car with tinted windows screeching up out front, spraying bullets.

The screen showing crime scene tape and the aftermath of the killing. Gibney saying the lone eyewitness couldn't ID the shooters, wasn't even sure of color of the car, calling it "a tinted-up white trash starter kit." The footage changed to the day after Dustin Bent's funeral, Gibney saying an anonymous tip led to the younger Bent, Reggie, getting swept up in a sting and facing some hard time for trafficking cocaine, possession of a handgun.

"Leaves the middle brother, Jerrel, running things, facing off with the Dreads stepping out of Scarlem, trying to lay claim to some Rexdale housing projects." Ted reached the knob, turning down Gibney, saying, "While you assholes throw headlines around like 'ghetto blasting' and 'spiking gun violence.'" Reaching for the bottle of scotch in his drawer, he filled a glass on the bureau, saying, "Here's to supply and demand."

Glancing at his TAG Heuer, he figured he'd wait till Bucky Showalter showed up out front before calling Jerrel Bent. Then he'd let Mal Rocca and his Pizza Connection know he'd have the rest of their money. Tossing back the scotch, he considered holding back an Uzi and sending Rocca his own message. Son of a bitch having his guy's finger hacked off like that. He refilled the glass.

"The way Mal fuckin' Rocca makes his point, showing you don't mess with him," Ted Bracey said on the phone, calling Mateo Cruz down in Poughkeepsie, letting him know he just got Bucky's call, ended up explaining what happened to his man Robbie Boyd, calling it, "An extensive fucking manicure."

"Doesn't look good. Your guy gets done like that, snatched up right out your front door, and you not doing nothing about it."

"I say I'm doing nothing?"

"Just saying, what it looks like."

"What it's supposed to look like. Shit's all gonna be in the rearview, don't you worry about it."

"Yeah, well, maybe till then, pack more than a lunch when you walk out the door."

Ted hung up, telling the receiver to fuck off.

Bonnie buzzing the intercom, telling him his ten o'clock was waiting.

"What ten o'clock?"

"Name's Jeff Nichols."

Remembering, Ted said, "Send him up."

... PRELUDE

Ted leaned across the desk. Silver hair parted and combed back, tailor-made suit, fancy watch, gold ring on his finger. He offered his hand, saying, "Marcel Banks tells me good things about you."

"Yeah, same here," I said. Tie around the guy's neck was worth more than everything I had on. Wanted to stick a finger in my own collar, the clip-on choking me. Felt every bit the aging ex-con in a cheap suit. I stopped my toe from playing with the hole in my sock. No point aggravating it.

A bureau was tucked next to the desk, one of them small Sony TVs, a gold clock on top, its pendulum swinging back and forth. A photo of a little league team on the wall, Bracey's AutoPark jerseys in blue and gold, championship plaque next to the clock. Sharing & Caring community awards. Bracey's AutoPark making a difference. Keeping it local.

"Place used to be a boxing gym called the Knockout," Ted said, starting with small talk.

"That right?" I glanced around, cinder blocks painted white, posters of Chuvalo on the walls, place like a shrine to the man.

"Never knocked off his feet," Ted said, glancing at the one behind me, above my head. "You ever see old George fight?"

"Never did, no, but know who he was."

"Is," Ted said. "Man's still around."

"Right. He still fighting?"

Ted shook his head, "Last one was back in '78. KO'd some guy down at the St. Lawrence."

I nodded. "He train here, old George?"

"Might've." He went on, telling me how he'd picked the place up at auction, had it gutted, the walls painted, floors sanded, open ducting and exposed beams at the ceiling, kept a few of the Chuvalos.

"Seen the ones in the showroom," I said, guessing they were important to him. "One with Ali behind the girl . . ."

"Bonnie, down at reception, right?" Ted explaining that before their match, Ali called George a washerwoman.

"Bet he didn't after, right?" I guessed.

"Bet your ass he didn't. Fifteen rounds, old washer-woman's still standing."

I glanced out the open door. The reception desk faced a line of sales desks on the showroom floor, Vick the only guy sitting there when I came in. Giving me a grin and a thumbs up. A bank of industrial windows next to him faced out onto St. Clair. Late-models lined the showroom floor, mostly Chevs and Fords.

Done with boxing tales, Ted went on about selling cars, not saying anything about running guns, the real reason Marcel sent me. Guess he was biding his time, making sure

I was right for it. Didn't tell him Marcel already filled me in, how the hidden cells opened.

The intercom buzzed, Ted clicking the button, Bonnie saying Robbie Boyd was back, Ted saying he was busy, switching it off, adjusting the smile, both of us hearing footsteps coming up the stairs. Then the door opened and the guy, Robbie Boyd, stood there, waving his bandaged hand, saying, "Fucking avoiding me now, Ted?"

"Robbie, my man, can see I'm in the middle, right?" Ted motioned to me, keeping his cool.

"Fuck that, you owe me."

"Already told you, what you got coming's coming. Look, Robbie, sorry about the mishap, but —"

"Mishap, fuck mishap, Ted. You got any idea of the pain?" Robbie waving his bandaged hand, letting me see it. Saying, to me, "Here's what happens, you work at a place like this, pal." The guy looking pissed.

"Maybe some guy that you sold a lemon," Ted said. "The thing crapped out on the DVP, and the guy took it personal." He leaned back, talking to Robbie, smiling at me, saying, "They're out there, right, the lunatics?"

Robbie said to me, "I were you, man, I'd run the fuck out of here." Waving the bandaged hand again. "That or stick a gun in your pants while you still got the fingers to pull the trigger." Then he turned and stomped down the steps, could hear him saying something to Vick on his way out.

I turned to Ted, saying, "That the guy I'm replacing?"

"Man's heart was never in the job."

"Fingers either, huh?"

Grinning back, he said, "So, Marcel says you got a hard bark."

"Yeah, but so far, we just been talking about boxing and selling cars."

"First things first," Ted said, putting the smile back on, "but, anything else, that part comes later."

"So, Vick tells me you two go back, the Don, right?"

"Vick's not holding back." I guessed Vick had sat in the same chair when he signed up. My toe was back to playing with the hole in the sock. Fuck it, I let it play. Stuck my finger in my collar, realized you can't loosen a clip-on tie.

"Why were you in?"

"Carelessness."

Ted Bracey smiled, acting like jailing was fun, then saying, "So we're clear, I go by gut. You tell me where you're going, not where you been."

"Meaning?"

"Meaning on the surface this job's about making sales, talking cars to customers. Anything else comes later. Sound like something you're up for?"

"So far, yeah."

Clicking the intercom, Ted said, "Bonnie, coffee." Then told me he had a broker buying up late-models at auction south of the border, New York State mostly. Lease-ends and repos, low mileage, clean and American made, nothing past two years old. Ted having the cars detailed at his shop in

Poughkeepsie, strapping them on a car-carrier and transporting them north.

Marcel Banks had told me most of the part Ted wasn't saying, Poughkeepsie being where they added the cells that opened on hydraulics, state-of-the-art smuggling gear according to Marcel. Every car rigged so you had to put your foot on the brake and turn the key at the same time, flip a switch under a fake bottom on the console, the hidden cells popping open, giving up its bellyful of guns.

"So, you want me selling cars, huh?"

"Ground level, same as Vick." Ted grinned. "Setup like this takes the right people, Jeff. Guys I can depend on."

I nodded. No problem with him being careful, the kind of thing that kept smart fellows out of places like the Don.

Opening the door, Bonnie brought in a service tray, setting it down, cups on saucers, a creamer and sugar bowl. A serious-looking woman with a chiseled smile, the definition of efficiency. Haircut blunt and clothes neat. She left without a word, closing the door behind her.

Stirring in a packet of sugar, I glanced at the clock on the bureau. Supposed to pick Ann up at the library over by Christie Pits in forty minutes, rain pattering against the high window behind Ted. Ted saying he paid twenty-five percent of profits, told me it was in my best interest to sell as close to sticker as I could. In case I couldn't, he set the mini at a hundred bucks, the least I'd make on a sale.

Glancing at his TAG Heuer, he said, "Little early, but I'm peckish. What say we grab a bite?" Didn't wait for an answer; he got up. "Deli next door's first-rate. Got the real kosher dills, you know the ones?"

I said yeah.

Reaching in his drawer, he pocketed what looked like a .32-cal Ruger. Saying nobody likes a car salesman, he took to the steps and crossed the showroom, telling Bonnie to hold his calls. I looked around, but Vick wasn't at his desk. Opening the door, Ted let me go first.

. . . BEAMSVILLE

Jamming the gears, Bucky Showalter hauled out of Lewiston, rolling onto the 405, then onto the QEW. His AM on some BTO and his thoughts on the truck stop this side of Port Dalhousie. The Dalhousie Delight served a six-inch stack, buttermilk cakes with blueberries and enough syrup a man could drown in. The waitress was Alicia, full-figured with a ready smile, all the woman a man could want, thinking about her as he flew along the highway.

Just Bucky's luck, the Beamsville scales' sign was flashing. Not even an hour from the Fort Erie crossing, Bucky guessing Ted Bracey's gal Bonnie got it wrong, the scales supposed to be closed this time of day.

Pulling in, he turned down the radio, the CB just giving squelch. Waiting on the long-haul ahead, he leaned back on the headrest, thinking ahead to a weekend of tipping up Heineken, thinking about the waitress. Way she felt, things she did lying there under him. When the long-haul ahead pulled back onto the highway, black diesel puffing from its stack, Bucky worked the stick, shifted and pulled the rig over the scale in the right lane. He waited, and then the signal light went red.

"Fuck me." Slapping both hands against the wheel.

Meant he had to pull in, the inspectors likely to bilk him for fuel tax or some shit. Coming from the booth, the guy in uniform signaled for Bucky to climb down. Swinging open his door, Bucky pointed to the inspection decal up on the windshield. Didn't hear the second guy coming from behind the trailer as he stepped down. Not suspecting anything but bureaucracy.

Cold-cocked from behind, he sunk to his knees. Felt the wet blood on the back of his head, Bucky tried to get up, getting hit again, a couple guys running past him, scrambling up on the trailer. Bucky lay there with his cheek on the pavement, the wet flowing along his ear. Last thing he was thinking, he was going to miss the sizzle of pancake batter hitting the grill. And the way the she felt — the waitress — fishing for her name as he spun into the dark. Katie, maybe that was it.

Deli-cious was filling fast, the noonday rush starting. Swivel stools at the long counter were all taken, a scattering of tables and a condiment counter lined the window. Ted laid his arms across the top of the of the corner booth, his back to the wall and his eye on the door. Rain slanted against the glass. A Federal Express truck splashed up water along St. Clair, pulling to the curb, the driver hitting his four-ways. People huddled under umbrellas walking past. Me, I was biting into a Rueben.

"You and Vick, like brothers in the joint, that kind of thing?"

"Saw him in the yard now and then, maybe the chow line. First I put eyes on him outside was at Marcel's, sitting in the next chair, saying, 'Hey brother, they let you out, huh?'"

Ted asking again what I did time for, liked that it was related to cars, telling me he had two cars jacked off the lot, grinning, saying if he ever caught a guy doing it, well, that's what the pistol was for, the one I saw him tuck in his jacket.

I smiled and asked about sales training.

"Use your instincts, go by gut. Tire kicker walks in looking at a ham sandwich, you sell him a Whopper with cheese, you follow?"

I nodded, said, "Yeah, I think so."

Pointing at the side dish, he said, "Sell me a pickle, same way you'd sell a car. Show me something."

"Sell you a dill from Hungary, tell you it's Polish, charge you extra." I dropped my crust on the plate.

He nodded. "It's the way you got to work the buyer, gain their trust, work the impulse. All the sales training you need."

The waitress came past, setting down our tab, looking annoyed at him, telling him he had a call, some guy named Mal, pointing to the wall phone by the counter. Reaching in his pocket, he handed her a five, said to tell Mal he wasn't here. Then he slapped a twenty on the tab without looking at it.

Tucking the five away, the waitress cleared the plates, pinched the twenty and the tab between two fingers and walked off.

It was the first time since I stepped through the Don's discharge area I could see the top of Shit Mountain, sure I was going to watch the shit rolling downhill for a change.

Getting up, Ted told me he had a trailer of late-models crossing at Lewiston, had a lot to do before it got here. Walking past the cash, he held the door and we walked to the car lot next door. A couple of Chevy vans and a 240Z Datsun sat around the side, a two-tone Challenger with stripes down the hood and *sold* written across the windshield. A pair of Fiestas sat on either side of the doors. Ted said he wanted me starting right away. "Things work out, we'll talk about an override, a little walking-around money."

"How about a draw?"

"Funny," Ted said. "Oh, one perk, the Quickie Wash . . ." Ted pointed west, could see part of the sign from here, saying it was his, too. Told me I could get a wash anytime I wanted, saying he liked his guys to roll around in clean cars, giving the right impression.

"Commission and a clean car, that's it, huh?"

"Any man worth his salt works for a cut, Jeff. Salary's for wimps. Sees a blower or grinder coming through that door, doesn't matter, a good salesman sees each one as an up, a sale in the making."

"Just, my old lady, she hears there's no regular pay . . ."

Ted stopped at the glass door and gave me a look. "You want to run it by the missus, that's fine by me. A man's got to appease the home front. Think I don't know? Trust me, man, I know."

I guessed he was letting my wheels of commerce cycle into motion. No ex-con was going to pass this up. Tugging open the door, he let me walk ahead. I guessed Ann had been waiting outside the library at Christie Pits about a half hour now.

Taking a couple of messages from Bonnie at reception, he introduced me as he looked at them and tossed them one by one in the wastebasket, wondering aloud what was taking Bucky. Going up the steps to his office, sitting behind the desk, he said, "I been in the trenches a long time, Jeff, and when something like this takes off . . ." He glanced at the ceiling, then took out some forms he wanted me to sign.

Folding his hands behind his head, he said, "Play it right, Jeff, you might get a shot at running things."

"Running things, huh?"

"Another part I'm not talking about. Be either you or Vick, the right man runs the show, the whole show . . ."

The phone rang, line one flashing, Ted waiting for Bonnie to buzz him, saying it was Bucky.

"Got to take this,"Ted said, offering me his hand, waiting till I went for the door. Pressing the button, saying, "Bucky, my man . . ."

Heard the rush of air and saw the color drain from his face as I closed the door.

. . . THE TWILIGHT REELING

The bricks of the library did little to shelter her from the slant of the rain. Pritchard, the head librarian, didn't like the staff hanging around inside after their shift, the old crow calling it loitering. Huddled in her jacket, Ann hugged the paper shopping bag close. Didn't need to tell me she was shivering, the slow burn over me being late the only thing keeping her warm. Her shoes looked soaked, her toes likely squelching water.

I swung the old Valiant Limited to the curb, catching the reflection in a window, my passenger-side headlight flickering like it had a tic. Took care not to splash water up at her.

Yanking the door, she got in and set the bag on the floor, saying, "I got popsicle toes." The bag starting to tear from being soaked, a tomato can poking through the bottom.

"Sorry, running a bit late."

"Forty-seven minutes."

I stopped myself from pointing to the red rocket stop just down the block.

"You couldn't call?"

"Middle of a job interview?" Flicking the heater on, I

said, "Couldn't be helped, Ann, you know that . . . but, I got good news."

She rubbed her wrinkled fingers in front of the vent. I checked the rearview; some guy in an Olds wagon the size of a rhino, with the woodgrain down the sides, tromped his pedal and cut me off, beating the light at Dufferin.

"Gonna ask how did it go?"

"Hear you better when my teeth stop rattling."

"Said I'm sorry."

"Some homeless guy comes by, asks if I'm okay. Had a spare Hefty bag in his shopping cart. Told me to just cut holes for my head and arms."

I smacked my horn at some delivery van that wouldn't yield, making my way up to St. Clair, pointing out the AutoPark as we passed.

"Okay, so tell," she said.

"Well, me and Ted, we hit it off."

"The one from the barber shop?"

"That's Vick. Ted owns the place, guy I went to see."

"And he offered you the job?"

"That and maybe a chance to run things." Seeing the neon sign coming up on the right, I put on my signal and turned into the Quickie Car Wash.

"Now what?"

"Getting a wash."

"Know it's raining, right?"

"One of the perks. Ted owns this place, too. Get a wash anytime I want." Rolling down my window halfway, I eyed the pock-faced attendant shuffling up. Feigning sobriety, the kid said, "Welcome to Quickie W-Wash, s-sir." Tongue

tripping on the consonants. "R-running a s-special today."
Pockmark steadying himself against my lime-green door,
scraggly wet hair and eyes like bloodshot pools, saying,
"Comes with hot w-wax, s-sir."

Looking up at the menu board, I said, "Yeah, let's go
with that."

"Th-that'll be . . . uh, call it f-f-five even." Pockmark
looking across at Ann, trying for a wink.

"Signs says three eight-five." I pointed at the board.

"Yeah, then you got your t-taxes and s-shit . . ."

"Oh, supposed to tell you I'm working at the AutoPark."

"Wha?"

"Working for Ted Bracey."

He narrowed his eyes at me.

"Guy that signs your check."

"S-small world, uh?" Pockmark holding out his hand.

Looking at his dirty upturned hand, I thought, fuck it. I
wasn't going to sweat the small stuff. Not anymore. Pulling
the lone five from my wallet, I let him take it.

Stepping back, Pockmark looked over the Valiant, the
rusted-through front quarter panel, telling me Quickie
Wash wasn't r-responsible for any d-damage. He went about
unscrewing the aerial and handed it to me. Going to the front
of the car, he waved me forward, guiding me onto the tracks.

Rolling up the window, I felt the track grab the tires,
being guided along, saying to Ann, "Hey remember that
time, you and me, at that car wash by the airport." Did
it the one time at the Malton Kleen 'n Shine, back when
we started going out. The boarded-up Seaway Restaurant
across the street.

"Back when Patsy Cline made the charts, still wore a two-piece back then."

"Call me sentimental."

"Heard the part about my freezing toes, right?"

"Maybe warm you up." I took off the clip-on tie, tossed it in back.

Her grinning, me too, liking that look in her eye.

"Come on, Jeff, here, really?"

I unclipped my seat belt and fumbled with hers. "Make up for the conjugal visits you missed."

"Always made me feel dirty, like somebody was —"

"Just kidding, Ann," I said. "Come on, only got a couple minutes."

Pockmark got back in his booth, getting out of the rain.

Stopping my hand, she looked in my eyes, then hit her door lock. She wriggled her hips down in the seat, fingers flipping at her buttons, lifting hips and pressing her jeans past her knees, thumbs inside the elastic of her undies, wiggling them down. Water spraying at the chassis.

I got a knee over the console, the emergency brake handle poking my thigh. She pressed a leg against the door handle, arching her back, telling me to hurry up.

It was that first time all over, first place that wasn't a bed. The old Valiant shuddered along the tracks, water jetting against its grill, hood and windshield. I got in position, my belt catching on the brake handle.

Pressing up, she said, "Rest's up to you."

The fronds swished and slapped the windshield, back and forth like tentacles.

"Bet Deb and Dennis never did something crazy like

this." Shaking the belt loose, I banged my head on the rearview.

Ann's knee knocked the glovebox open, her elbow popping the door lock, the two of us nearly tumbling out. Water and soap gushing, the fronds slapping at us.

Ann yelling, "Ow," as I shut the door on her hair, having to open and re-shut it.

Laughing, she pushed me away. It was over.

Getting over in my seat, I looked out the windshield as the fronds stopped, the dryer coming on. Both of us arching and zipping up.

"Rain check?" she said.

"You bet."

The two of us laughing.

Straightening her clothes, she said, "Okay, so, what about this job?"

The Valiant was tugged along, the hot wax spraying the rockers and grill.

"Well . . . can tell you we're moving up."

"Yeah, how far?"

"Right up there."

"Come on, how much?"

Looking out the window, seeing the exit coming, I tried to sell it.

. . . THE SHILLY SHALLY

"You fucking me?" A trace of Kingston in the voice, Jerrel Bent set his forearms on Ted's desk, the bull shoulders under the tailored pinstripes, doctor bird tie pin, his deep-set eyes burning, like this white boy was talking shit to him. Shaved head and a broad nose.

Easing back in the leather, Ted glanced at the black muscle filling the door, neither of them big, but both looking serious. Ted betting there were pistols under the jackets. James "Dirty Leg" Freeze with a goatee and the stone killer look, and Errol "Blue Eyes" Ealy. Lighter skinned, leaning on the door frame, looking easy. Ted could make out the Suburban outside the showroom doors.

"You'll get your guns." Ted tried again, telling Jerrel how the trailer got jacked at the Beamsville scales. Assholes posing as inspectors jumped his man Bucky, must have known about the guns. "Fuckers cleaned us out."

"Not us, you." Jerrel stabbing a big finger at the air, big square ring with a diamond in the middle.

"And I'll make it right."

"No doubt about that," Jerrel said.

"I find out who did it —"

Jerrel put up his hand, didn't want to hear it.

"You'll get your guns, got my word."

"I'm gonna have more than your word if you don't get them." Jerrel thumped his fist, the sound like a pail of cement dropping on the desk. Getting up, he walked out. Blue Eyes and Dirty Leg following, looking over at Vick as they crossed the showroom floor, Blue Eyes making a finger gun, giving him a smile and dropping his thumb like a hammer.

Closing the drawer on his Saturday night special, Vick watched until the Suburban pulled away. His wink telling Bonnie everything was alright. Heard Ted barking for more coffee.

"I told you . . ." Ann's eyes lost the laughter, flashed electric.

The dryer overhead had just switched off, its roar dying down, the Valiant shaking off the conveyer, the passenger-side headlight blinking on and off, reflecting in the exit sign.

"And I told you I'd see him, hear him out. Go from there." I drew back, shrugged like that was that.

"I thought we'd talk first."

"Was an on-the-spot thing, Ann."

"On-the-spot, huh?" And she let a wild one fly, her slap blocked by the mirror. Clutching her hand, she cried out, growled in pain.

"Jeez, take it easy." Straightening the mirror, I looked at her, the veins in her temples throbbing.

"Take it easy. Pipe dreams and promises, Jeff. That's the best you got." Spittle at the edge of her mouth. Shaking the sting from her hand, she pressed her fingers between her thighs. "You're a piece of work, you know it?"

"Maybe we'll talk when you calm down." I rolled for the exit, thinking if she swung at me again, she'd be walking home, rain or no rain, this librarian going postal, needing a Quaalude or something stronger.

Snapping on her lap belt, she did her Zen breathing, sniffing through her nose, puffing through her mouth. The funk of Swift's mixed with that of Canada Packers, the fat of Hogtown lingering in the face of gentrification.

Glaring at me, she said, "How about we flip, see who's gonna blow the landlord this month." More sniffing and puffing. Using an incisor like a file, she trimmed the broken nail hanging from her finger, one she just painted with the new color, watermelon.

"Take it easy," I repeated. Ann spitting a bit of nail at me.

No point talking to her when she was like this, Ann needing a couple glasses of burgundy to settle. Pulling from the car wash, I merged eastbound without looking first.

The Civic in the outside lane screeched its brakes, the car jerking, the driver leaning on the horn, letting it blare.

Cranking down her window, fast as she could turn the handle, Ann clicked off her lap belt and pulled herself halfway out of the window, twisting onto the roof and yelling, "One toot, lady. All you effing need. You got it?"

Eyes bugging behind corrective lenses, the elderly Civic driver turned her wheel. Gunning a U-turn in heavy traffic, crossing double lines and streetcar tracks, the old woman nearly clipped a Suburban with tint all the way around. The bray of horns and screeching rubber enveloped the block, and the old woman wouldn't make the seniors' center this day. The lunatics were out here, and she was heading home to tell her hubby the second seal had been broken and the red horse had ridden forth.

A young couple behind their stroller stopped and stared in disbelief. Ann climbed back in, asking what they were looking at, rolling up the window, leaving the couple with enough suppertime talk for many a night to come: the erosion of social grace and the type of world they had delivered a child into.

The Quickie Wash attendant watched from the booth, firing up a roach and puffing smoke.

The grey van pulled up next to me, the passenger and driver looking over, a Maltese cross dangling from their rearview. I looked back at the two guys, knowing that look.

"We agreed, no commission," Ann said, buckling up again.

"You agreed. Look, I got the job, Ann. Ask me, you ought to be smiling." Glaring ahead, I could feel the two guys in the van still looking over. Flicking on the radio, I got Bro Jake doing the Champ on the Q.

"So, like, I'm supposed to be happy?" Ann not leaving it alone, switching the radio off.

"Not gonna land some Ivy League job, Ann. I stay on the straight and narrow, I gotta take what I can get."

"What, jobs for victims?" Filing the broken nail with her tooth, she didn't notice the two guys in the van. It pulled ahead and turned left at the next side street.

"Give it a chance, Ann, you'll see. It's a good career move."

"Good move?" She stomped her foot, her shoe squishing water, her arms locking across her chest, keeping herself from taking another swipe at me, saying, "The only move you're gonna see's when I start packing."

. . . ALL THE BELLS AND WHISTLES

"Set your dogs on me, Mal. Hacking my guy's finger, the ones that feed my family. How you want me to be, happy?" Ted Bracey was talking into the phone, knowing he needed to buy time with Mal Rocca, the loan shark who put up the cash for the dealership, getting serious about collecting it back. Ted with no idea who hit his car-carrier at the Beamsville scales. Somebody knowing how to get the guns from the hidden cells. Bucky Showalter was laid up in West Lincoln with a dozen stitches across his skull.

"Just letting you know where we stand," Mal Rocca said, "what happens you try to screw with me."

"Nobody's screwing with nobody. The points you're charging . . . man, talk about screwing."

"Another thing," Mal said, "I'm tacking on two more."

"Points? You fucking kidding me?"

"You got till end of the week, show me something." Then he hung up.

Looking at the receiver, Ted gritted his teeth and squeezed its neck, then smacked it into the cradle, banged it till a piece of Bakelite flew off.

Sitting there, he thought things through till Bonnie buzzed up, telling him there was a Mateo Cruz on two. Unclenching his jaw, Ted stabbed at the button.

Mateo said, "The fuck's going on?" Said he just heard from Bucky.

"That fuck Rocca's tacking on two points."

The line went dead.

Hammering the receiver down, Ted swept the phone off the desk. Taking his Ruger from the drawer, he pointed at the phone, the damned thing beeping, letting him know it wasn't hung up right. For a second, he felt like shoving the barrel against his own tonsils. Finally dropping it back in the drawer, he reached for the phone, told it to shut up and hung it up, then reached the bottle in his drawer and buzzed Bonnie back, told her, "Coffee."

The next call was to the escort service, Ted trying to remember the redhead's name, needing something to calm his mind.

... FRICTION CITY

Slinging the grocery bag on the counter, the soggy paper tearing open, Ann walked from the kitchen, said she was going to run a bath, the hot water bound to do her good. Leaving me to unpack. A can of Libby's rolled and dropped to the floor.

Picking up the dented can, I said I could fix her a tea. I looked down at my toe poking through the sock.

"Need something stronger," she called.

"Wine?" Reaching the box of burgundy, I shook it, thinking who puts a box back with only a few drops in it. Remembering it was me.

"Just surprise me the way you do."

Maybe a bath would melt her mood. I pulled out a sack of frozen fries, glancing at the ingredients. Not even real potatoes, worse than the slop in the Don.

The knock at the front door had me jumping. Tossing the fries in the freezer, I got set for the Jehovahs, same two guys had been working the block with the latest *Watchtower*. Go ahead, try and shove a shoe in my door and see what happens. Eye to the peephole, I was looking at a fisheye

Tibor Kovach, the guy from next door. Guy who moved into the next semi the same day Ann moved in here. Started arguing about my car blocking the spot where he wanted to park his moving van and pull down the ramp in back. I told him I'd been living here two years, parked it in the same spot every day. Seeing how he was new, he could turn his moving truck around, pull the ramp down facing the other way. I shut the door on him, and we didn't say much to each other before I got sent up. Ann living here alone, keeping up the rent. First day I got out, Tibor's back over here accusing me of selling grass to his kid, Dmitri. Caught the kid rolling a joint, sitting in his Firebird on my boulevard, taking my spot. Confiscating the weed, he came over, showed me the joint, figured since I was an ex-con, the kid got it from me. Tibor asking what I had to say about it. Told him the thing looked like the kid was wearing mittens when he rolled it, pot falling out both ends, a stem sticking through the Zig-Zag. Then he went on about my unruly hedge, called me an idiot, and walked away before I could slam the door.

"Hedge still blocking view," Tibor said now, pointing to the tangle of blackberry-lashed cedar down by the street.

"Told you last time, I'd run it by the landlord," I said, looking past him, a grey van rolling by, pretty sure it was the same one from out front of the Quickie Wash, recognized the cross on the mirror. The same two guys looking this way. Maybe they were cops, keeping an eye, ex-cons always on their radar, guilty of some shit or other.

"You live here, not landlord," Tibor said.

"Yeah, how about this, I cut it the day little Dmitri stops parking his clunker in my spot? How'd that be?" I pointed

57

to the ruts on my boulevard.

"Grass is dead and boulevard belong to city."

"Yeah, and hedge belongs to the landlord."

Tibor pressed his nose against the screen, huffing, looking like he was coming through the mesh, telling me to keep away from Dmitri.

"Your kid, how about you tell him?"

He said if only we were in Minsk, pointing a fat finger and throwing in, "Wife say is no reasoning with you."

"Yeah, the little woman finally get a green card, huh?" I said, Tibor living next door on his own, just him and his kid and a mangy dog.

"Not my wife, your wife," Tibor said.

The van rolled past the opposite way now, both guys still looking over.

"Hey, my man, since we're talking, how about you keep your mutt out of my trash? Tired of cleaning it up."

"Don't blame Sasha, *govnó*." Tibor pulled back his nose, left a dent in the mesh, the man's hands balled at his sides, saying, "You put trash out in morning," Pointing around to the neighbors, he said, "then raccoon don't knock down at night." Turning away before he did something that would get his resident status revoked, he headed for his yard, calling over his shoulder, "Back in Minsk, I choke shit from you, drag you in the Svisloch."

"Svisloch, what's that, a dish?" Looking at the street past the brambles, I shut the door and threw on the bolt. Taking the burgundy from the pantry, I held it up and shook the last of the wine into my mouth. Then I filled the kettle, put it on a burner.

... THE MAGNIFYING SIDE

Careful not to spill, I opened the bathroom door and set Ann's tea on the vanity. Banging her fists in the bubbles, she slid down into them, saying, "Lord, take me now." I remembered her telling me head librarian Pritchard once claimed it was impossible to drown oneself. Looked like Ann was considering the challenge.

Going back to the kitchen, I sat at the table, thinking I should go get some more wine, picking at the Formica and staring at the clock until I heard her step out. Ann taking her jeans off the door hook, saying, "Please, legs, fit." Sucking in air, she pulled the jeans up, cursed and forced them over her hips. Coming out with her hair wet, she walked past, her makeup mirror in her hand.

I watched her set it on the window sill in the dining room, aiming the magnifying side at Tibor's place. "What are you doing?" I asked.

"A little Feng Shui trick, watch and learn. Reflecting that jerk's piss-poor attitude right back at him. Magnified, ten effing fold."

"Poor bastard won't know what hit him, huh?" I said,

water gurgling in the Feng Shui fountain on the dining hutch, a twin of the one she'd been saving in case I got a job with a desk. The thing supposed to harness good chi, the fountain apparently bubbling with it.

Coming into the kitchen, she stood behind me, her hands working the back of my neck, her way of letting me know we were okay again.

. . . ON THE CHIN

Past the bramble hedge, Bundy Olich and Egg Araz sat watching the hopped-up Firebird pull up with its tailpipes grumbling, parking in front of Nichols's house, tight behind the shitbox Valiant. Bundy catching a glint of light reflecting from the dining room window. Saying he didn't like it.

Egg turned and looked at him.

"There." Bundy pointing at the flash of light, seeing the kid get out of the muscle car and walk to the house next door.

Egg gave Bundy the look, bottom lip hanging open.

"Could be coming off a rifle scope or something, for all we know," Bundy said. Mal Rocca had told them this loser, Jeff Nichols, had done a stretch in the Don, just released and working for Ted Bracey. "The kind of guy who could get a street gun." Looking at Egg, his dumb, open mouth.

"Got a feeling, that's all. Could be trouble's all I'm saying," Bundy said, "maybe not a pushover like the other guy, Robbie what's-his-name."

Egg shrugged, flicked a finger at the dangling cross, thinking nothing they couldn't handle. His own piece in a shoulder rig. Mal Rocca was paying them to do a job, Egg intended to get it done. Ted Bracey had one more week. He didn't pay up, the two of them would come for this ex-con and send him back in parts.

Bundy saying, "And what's with going for the little guy. I mean, first this Robbie guy, just a working stiff. This deadbeat Bracey's making excuses, not paying up. You ask me, why not go after him, the guy who owes. Take one of his fingers."

That got the lower lip closing, Egg pursing it over his top lip.

"Guess Mal figures 'cause this Bracey's the one who owes," Bundy said, "maybe needs the fingers, you know, for counting off the dough. Cut one of his guys instead, maybe you send a bigger message." He gave a shrug, saying, "Guess, who gives a fuck." Seeing the glint from the window again, Bundy said, "How about we back the fuck up? Like a fucking sitting duck out here."

Turning the key, Egg took the shift in his fist, sticking it in R, turning to look out the back, backing along the shoulder.

. . . HOT STEPPIN'

Tapping his pen on the desk blotter, Vick DuMont sat there bored out of his skull. Eyes out the showroom window. Hated making follow-up calls and waiting for walk-ins, the tire kickers balking over sticker prices, not believing a word he said. One guy came in yesterday, betting they rolled the odometers back, then bitched about the price, busting Vick's balls.

Looking at the Chuvalo poster up over Bonnie's desk, the guy looking fierce with the leather gloves up, Vick grinned, remembering Ali calling him the washerwoman. Then old George showing up at some press conference dressed up like one. After just losing one to Terrell, and having only seventeen days to prep for the fight, Chuvalo made one hell of an underdog. Vick getting a good feeling and taking some bookie's seven-to-one action on Chuvalo just making the distance. Slapping down five hundred. Vick coming away, counting the three and a half Gs in his hand.

Feeling a bit like the underdog himself after Ted gave Jeff Nichols the spare office after his first week. Ted saying it was on account of Jeff's experience with cars, nothing personal. Didn't make sense to Vick. Jeff doing time for jacking them, nothing to do with selling them. Made Vick feel a little better since leaking the info about the car shipment to Randy Hooper.

"So, this stuff really works?" Bonnie asked, sitting at the reception desk, looking at the sample box of Maxx, then at the sales flyer, the before-and-after shots, asking how he knew for sure which was before and which was after. Bonnie not believing everything she read.

"Think I'd waste my time if it didn't?" he said, looking over from his sales desk, adding, "Tell you what, take a box home to Allen, see for yourself."

Taking the bottle from the box, she uncapped it and sniffed, reeling back, the smell like a slap. "Oh, my God."

"Powerful, huh? Means it works."

A smell like it came from the glands of a skunk. Bonnie closing the box. "No way Allen's going around like that." No amount of Brut would mask it.

"Shower cap in the box, locks in the smell. But still, long after the smell, Alan's got all his hair back. Maxx is the real deal, Bonnie. My hand to God."

Hawking Maxx on the side for Jackie Delano since his release, Vick had been hoping to get back into Jackie's pants. The woman not much to look at, but made up for it in other ways. It was Jackie who met the inventor of the stuff down in Santiago. Some vacation she went on. Jackie thinking she could make some real money back home, maybe sell the formula to Revlon or an outfit like that down the road. Vick getting onboard early, committing himself before finding out she'd been hooking up with Randy Hooper the whole time he was serving his stretch in the Don.

Saying she'd have to think about it, Bonnie shoved the box away from her and took an incoming call.

Tapping his pen on the desk blotter, Vick outlined the year on top of the calendar, inking in the holes of 1986. Vick was thinking about getting some sun, still had that prison pallor, skin looking like an old potato. Ought to grab a bag of takeout and head to the Beaches, check out the chicks along the boardwalk.

Bonnie called over, "Line one, Jimmy from Uxbridge."

Pressing the blinking button, Vick picked up and said yeah, told Jimmy from Uxbridge the Granada was still on the lot, Jimmy saying stick shift wasn't his first choice, not fussy on the color either, asking if there was wiggle room on the price. Vick told him there was always wiggle room, saying, "You drop down before five, I'll throw in floor mats and a free car wash for a year." Getting bored with Jimmy's umming and awwing, Vick looked out the window.

A rusty bucket slowed on St. Clair, a Maverick, the kind of crate his nanna used to go to church in. The passenger window rolled down and a gun barrel stuck out. Tossing the phone, Vick yelled "Down" and was diving for the floor, the showroom glass bursting, bullets punching into the cars and desks and walls. Pennants outside were shredded and dropping like confetti. Bonnie was jumping around and screaming, hands to her head. Crawling, then springing at her, Vick tackled her behind the reception desk.

When it stopped and he was sitting up, looking at the

shards of glass sticking from his bloody palms, he asked, "You okay?"

Her mouth trembled and she was crying, but she was okay. Aftermath dust hung in the air. Holes pocked everything and busted glass lay everywhere. The Coke machine bled, a couple tires were hissing air. Vick could smell the Maxx, the bottle shattered on the desk, the smell mingling with what was wafting in from the meatpackers a block away.

Bonnie stayed hunched and hung onto him. The howl of a siren sounded along St. Clair.

"Okay, maybe I got a bit carried away at the car wash," Ann said, leaning on the door frame of the spare bedroom/office.

"A bit?" I said, looking up from the Black Book, boning up on aftermarket car values. It had been a week, and we hadn't talked about the fight.

"Understand what I been through, with you being locked up. Barely making the rent, lonely all the time," she said. "Anyway, guess it's good, them giving you an office." Her leg showed from behind her pink housecoat.

"Told you it would work out."

Then she grinned. "You believe that woman, honking at us like that?"

"You gave her the finger."

She shrugged.

"How about the couple with the stroller?" I was shaking my head, thinking of her hanging out the window, yelling at the old woman.

"How about you never mind, and come to bed," Ann said, saying it was past midnight.

Slapping the Black Book closed, a long night of getting familiar with car values, learning the ropes. I tossed it on the copy of the Kelley Blue Book. Read a couple chapters of some book I had Ann get from the library: The Science of Getting Rich. Showing Ted I had the stuff to run the AutoPark.

The phone/fax machine on the floor gave that short ring, the fax clicking, bleating and printing.

"Who calls this late?" Looking at the electrostatic paper curling from the machine, she asked, "What's this?" watching the before-and-after shots for Maxx drop into the tray.

"Vick again," I said. "Guy's hawking this stuff on the side, supposed to grow hair, calls it a miracle cure."

Ann taking the fax from the tray and reading, looking at the before-and-after likeness of Archie the Elvis.

Scrawled in pen at the top: Where were you when hell broke loose? Taking it from her, I frowned, saying, "Guy's a drama queen." No idea what he was talking about, I said, "Guess I should call."

"Can't wait till morning, huh?" she said, showing more leg, flapping the housecoat closed, then turning for the door.

Balling the fax, I tossed it at the trash and switched off the lamp, guessing she was ovulating and we were finishing what we started at the Quickie Wash. Vick could wait.

. . . THE POLYESTER SHUFFLE

Bullet hole through the hollow-core office door, another one just missed Chuvalo hanging over my desk. An emergency crew had boarded up the front windows, just the overhead fluorescents lighting the showroom. The desk computer had been spared. I set the Zen desk fountain next to it. Ann had bought two for the price of one at Honest Ed's, giving me one for the new office, saying it was for luck.

A half hour of talking to the detectives, and I sat back, closed my eyes and swiveled in the leather chair, trying to make sense of the place getting shot up. Both cops sure that me and Vick being ex-cons had something to do with it. Asked if I pissed anybody off in the joint.

The tap at the door had me thinking the cops had more questions. Robbie Boyd stood in the doorway with his hand still wrapped up, the guy who'd been yelling at Ted the day I landed the job.

"You didn't run, huh?" he said, stepping in and looking around, eyes stopping on the fountain next to the IBM computer. "Hell is that?"

"A Zen thing."

Taking the envelope Ted had left with me, the one with Robbie Boyd's name on it, I said, "Figured I'd stick around, see what happens."

Robbie took it and looked the check over, tucking it away, saying, "Guy puts on a show, tells you what you want to hear. By the time you figure it out . . ." Robbie lifted the hand, showing it to me.

I heard the plywood door open out front, and Ted and Vick walked across the showroom. Vick juggling a coffee tray, raising the brows when he saw Robbie.

Robbie saying to Ted, "Still owe people money, huh?"

"Got yours, right, Robbie, what you came for?" Ted said, sounding cold.

Robbie nodded at me. "Don't say I didn't warn you." Giving Vick a high five with the good hand, telling him not to be a stranger, he went down the steps, going past Bonnie's shot-up reception desk and out the door.

"Good people, ones that stick by you, damned hard to find," Ted said, parking his butt on the corner of my desk.

"Yeah, 'specially when the bullets start flying." Vick set the coffee tray next to Ted, taking a cup. Looking at me, saying, "What's your story? Didn't get my memo?"

"Got to bed early, not that it's any of your business."

"You get any kind of a look?" Ted said to Vick.

"Was busy diving for the floor."

Ted took a coffee, peeled the lid and looked into it a long moment, then said, "Don't mind you boys knowing . . . had to borrow heavy to get this place running."

"No shit," Vick sat in the spare chair, peeling back his lid, saying, "Borrowed from the wrong loan shark, huh? Maybe missed paying the vig?"

"Didn't exactly walk into the Commerce Bank," Ted said.

Shaking a packet of Sweet'N Low, Vick ripped into it and said, "Wasn't no loan shark shot up the place."

"Had to see something, desk right at the window," Ted said.

"What I told the cops, Ford pulls up, window rolls down, some clown starts shooting."

"Make the plate?" Ted said.

"Gun barrel comes out a window, I'm diving for floor. Every fucking time, brother."

"Way the cops tell it, you likely saved Bonnie's life, some kind of hero."

"Yeah well, woman was slow reading the situation."

"Should mention," I said, "got a couple guys dogging me last couple days."

"Rocca's guys. I'll get him some money, take care of it," Ted said.

"Maybe you need to sweeten things up here, too, uh?" Vick said.

Ted looked at him, then at me. "Just gave you an office, right?"

"Old lady takes a swipe every time I walk through the door," I said, "points at the stack of bills."

"Promise you boys'll be taken care of. Got my word."

"Yeah, how about you lay it out, all of it," Vick said. "Always good to know who's shooting at you."

Ted thought a moment, then said, "Like I said, I owe

this guy, Mal Rocca. Got a bit behind, and guess he's getting antsy."

"So he sends the guys did Robbie?" Vick said.

"Same guys tailing me," I said.

"Said I'll take care of it." Ted explaining he was buying more cars, had them coming north. Be another shipment next week. "You boys hang in, you can take your pick, company cars fresh off the carrier. Chevy or Ford, whatever you want. How's that?"

"Fuck Ford and fuck Chevy," Vick said, "how about you toss in a couple of Smith & Wessons?" He pulled his smokes, found a match and lit up, tossed the spent match in my fountain, saying, "Doesn't answer who shot up the place."

Finishing his coffee, Ted got off the desk, looking at his TAG Heuer, saying he had a guy from the insurance stopping by soon.

"Yeah, you covered for drive-bys?" Vick said.

"Gonna find out," Ted said. "Meantime, there's some twelve-year-old in my drawer. Bottle didn't take a bullet, you boys are welcome to a snort." Then he was gone.

Vick looked at me, popping his brows, saying he could use one.

. . . IN-LAW OUTLAW

After the phone call to NOR-AM for new windows, Ted flipped through the Grand & Toy catalog, picked out a new reception desk. The College Pro crew were set to come in and patch, prime and paint next week. The insurance adjuster acting like Father Christmas. Then Ted placed an ad in the *Star* for a new receptionist, Bonnie telling him she quit. He left us the scotch bottle, said he was going home, calling it a hell of a day.

"He squares up with this Mal Rocca guy, and maybe we get somewhere," I said.

"Doesn't tell us who shot holes in the place." Knocking his drink back, Vick slapped down the glass and said he had a strategy meeting over Maxx with Jackie. Left me sitting behind my desk. Ann's Feng Shui desk fountain gurgling water. I reached the box of Cohibas. Ted calling them Esplendidos, the kind Churchill smoked, giving us each a box and a cutter, calling it a bonus. Vick calling it danger pay.

Taking one, I ran it under my nose. Smelled like earth. Rolling it between my fingers, I peeled the wrapper, sticking it in my mouth, trying to convince myself my train had come into the station. Soon my ass would be sitting in a German car, socks with no holes and Gucci shoes on my feet, watching a Japanese console TV. Long way from the eight-by-ten cell, the smell of the guy in the next bunk, a toilet with no lid. Yeah, this was working out, if I didn't get shot first. I sat there drinking Ted's scotch. With an inch in the bottom of the bottle, I must have nodded off for a while. I woke with a kink in my neck. No idea how long I slept.

Snipping the cigar's end with the cutters, I poured the last of it and lit up, thinking I should call Ann, tell her I was running late.

Putting it off, I puffed, blowing smoke rings, my mind on the sex of last night, reliving it when the plywood door rattled. I looked up as two guys shouldered their way in, clomping into the showroom — the two guys from the grey van. Rough-looking, with size. The one in front had a square jaw, the other one held a boom box under one arm. Looking up at the light coming from my office, they walked to the steps.

"We're closed, fellas." No point saying it, but I got up, looking around for something to swing. Laying the cigar on the edge of my desk.

Looking around the shot-up place, making sure we were alone, they came past the cars and up the steps. The one holding the boom box closed my door, setting the stereo on my desk.

"Whatever you boys are selling . . ."

"Not selling, delivering," the guy with the dirty-blond hair said he was Bundy, calling the other one Egg, looking at the Chuvalo, then the desk fountain, saying, "Fuck's that?"

"Supposed to bring me luck." I picked up the cigar-cutter, playing with it.

"Taking over for Robbie Boyd, huh?" He reached the garden pruners from his pocket, grinning at my cigar-cutter, saying, "Guess mine's bigger, uh?"

"Makes you feel better," I said.

"Thing is, guy you work for owes the guy we work for."

"Ought to talk to him then."

"How about you give him a message?" Taking a step, he flipped off the safety catch. Taking the cigar from the edge of the desk, he hacked it with the parrot jaws and tossed the bits away, coming around the desk.

I threw the scotch bottle, glass bursting against the wall. Both of them ducking, I grabbed the landline and swung the base at him.

Blocking with a forearm, the blond guy got his arm tangled in the cord and snipped it, batting the phone across the floor, shoving me into the wall.

Sucking wind, I spidered my palm at his crotch, squeezing his boys, raking my instep down his shin. I threw a left, then hooked a right. But the guy had size on me, wading through it, catching me with a head butt. Grabbing a fistful of hair, he twisted me around, and I saw the desk rushing up. My head slammed into it. I fought to stay conscious.

Finding a wall plug, the other guy connected the boom box, thumbing the play button. Giving some volume, he started clomping some dance moves in construction boots, his laces untied. Nena singing about red balloons.

Bending me backwards across the desk, the one called

Bundy pressed an elbow into my windpipe and swung a leg, pinning my shoulders. Trying to pull a finger from my fist.

Throwing a pretty good elbow, I felt his cartilage snap, blood gushing from his nose. Cupping it, he looked at the blood dripping through his fingers. Pissed off now, he stabbed the pruners, and I jerked right, the guy gouging a trench into the oak. I caught him with a shovel hook, knocking him to the floor. Kicking, I caught some chin as he rose up. I jumped for the door. He caught an ankle from behind, got up and swung me into the wall, smashing his fist into my kidneys, bulldogging me back across the desk, flipping me and pinning me. Pressing down, he was yanking at my pants. Blood dripped from his face, angry eyes letting me know I was going to lose more than a finger.

Flat on the desk with the shit music blaring, I tried to twist free. A voice calling over the music.

The one with the boom box stopped dancing, pressed pause, the two of them looking at each other.

"You okay, Jeff?" Vick's voice from outside the door.

Easing his grip, Bundy guy got up, called back, "We're closed."

Egg cracked the door, enough to look out.

Vick stood with a cockeyed woman at the bottom of the steps, Vick with the lug-nut kit from the trunk of a Chevy. The woman with a heaped updo that made her about his height. She held a Duo-Tang stuffed with pages. Taking the wheel wrench, Vick handed her the extension.

Unplugging the boom box, Egg scooped it under an arm, like they were done here.

"Your lucky day, asshole." Wagging a finger at me, looking at the Chuvalo, Bundy swiped at the blood on his face, said, "To be continued." Looking at Vick and the woman, he followed his buddy out of the showroom, the splintered door slapping shut behind them.

Hands shaking, I straightened myself up, smiling at Vick, saying, "Sure glad you came back, brother."

"Man, I leave for an hour . . ."

"All in the timing," I said, holding out my hand, glad I still had fingers to shake his hand.

. . . BRAINSTORMING

"The fuck was that?" Vick said.

"Bracey's past catching up, the one he's not talking about." My hands shook as I sank into my chair.

The cockeyed woman went back through the showroom and secured the plywood door, hit some light switch, the fluorescents letting her look around at the shot-up cars. Stepped over the drying puddle of Coke, she came back up the steps.

Running a finger across the gouge in the desk, Vick looked at the chopped cigar, the cut phone cord, saying, "Ought to try the soft sell next time."

"Fuck next time," I said. "But I got to say again, I sure like your timing, my man."

"Swung back to show Jackie some bullet holes, point to where I took a dive, saved Bonnie's ass, how it went down. That and use the Xerox. Hoping it didn't take a bullet."

Telling him the copier was fine, I looked at the woman coming back into the office, cockeyed with the B52s hairdo. Not sure which eye to look at.

"Two of us used to be a thing," Vick threw in.

"Ex-thing," Jackie said, giving a nicotine smile and offering her man-hand across the desk, saying her name.

"Yeah, nice to meet you, Jackie." The woman had a construction grip, but still, I was never happier to see anybody in my life.

Straightening the chair on the far side, she wedged her hips between its arms.

Setting the tire iron against the jamb, Vick perched on the desk, pulling a bent smoke from behind an ear, frisking himself for a match.

From out in the showroom, the phone rang. Jackie reaching for my phone on the floor, seeing the cut cord, putting it on the desk. Straightening the shade, she set the lamp back on the bureau.

I went down to the reception desk, thinking it could be Ted, wanting to tell him what the fuck was going on. Picking up the receiver and pressing line one.

"Hey ya, sweetie." Ann's voice, saying she could keep dinner warm, started telling me what she didn't have on under the pink housecoat.

"Yeah, alright, how about you hold that thought, huh?" Thinking she was still ovulating, looking at my shaking hand, my heart still racing.

"Got somebody there?"

"Yeah, sorry about dinner, burning the midnight oil, kinda in the middle of things." Saying I'd call back, I hung up and went back to the office.

Striking a match on his thumbnail, Vick lit up, the Feng Shui water fountain making a suitable ashtray.

Pulling one from a pack of Pall Malls, Jackie told him

to light her up. Leaning close, he touched his to hers, the woman puffing it to life.

Vick flicked ash in the fountain and slid it over, sloshing water, so she could get to it. Jackie puffing and flicking ashes.

"So, these the guys did Robbie, coming for us one at a time?" Vick said.

"Said something about Ted paying what he owed."

"Till he does, you ought to pack more than that," Vick said, nodding at the cigar-cutter, lifting his shirt to show the butt of a pistol. Vick saying he brought Jackie along to introduce us, hoped to talk about Maxx and get me on board. "Pay's good, plus it's a hell of a lot safer."

"The hair thing again, huh?"

"Yeah, the hair thing. See, we been brainstorming," Vick said, "rethinking our approach. Got some new ideas. Thought we'd run it by you, get your two cents."

"Well, sure glad you showed up when you did."

"Maybe it's a sign. Anyway, this thing's solid gold, plus Jackie here's a whiz with the whole marketing bit."

"That right?" I looked at her, the Ronald McDonald updo, the woman reaching a box of Maxx from her bag and setting it on the desk. Picking it up like I was interested, I turned the box and read the label.

"Worked the hair trade back in the day," she said. "Fluke luck that I met this guy on a trip to Santiago, guy mixing the stuff in his sink and selling it to the locals."

Taking the bottle from the box, uncapping it, I reeled back from the smell. "Holy smokes."

"Strong, uh? I know, but you ought to see the hair on the locals," she said.

"Thought I faxed you a memo," Vick said. "Product info, before-and-afters and all that."

"Must've missed it," I said, looking back to her. "So, the hair trade, huh? You like with Revlon, Clairol, a place like that?"

"Worked the Do or Dye, crazy busy place in Cabbagetown."

"Cabbagetown, huh?" Practically across the river from the Don Jail.

"Should've seen it on weekends," she said. "Gone now, but man, back in the day . . . four chairs going strong nine to five. Worked another place after by the Ports of Call. Called the Chop Shop. Heard of it?"

"Can't say so." Had a place we called that up in Malton, place I used to drop off hot cars.

She took her folder of papers, went back down the steps, behind Bonnie's desk, making photocopies, Vick said something about the two guys with the shit music coming back, maybe bringing more guys and bigger clippers. "Maybe we ought to split."

"Not a bad idea." Fishing in the drawer for my keys, I thought I'd call Ted when I got home, ask him about those Smith & Wessons.

Jackie finished with the machine, turned it off, and kept on talking about marketing Maxx on the way out, going on about the shotgun method.

"Shotgun, huh?"

"Yeah, we go off in all directions, but keep a focus on the hair trade. Stuff's got to speak to people."

"Yeah, and what's it got to say?"

Touching her hive, she said, "Thick, sexy hair."

Switching off the lights, I pulled the plywood door as tight as I could, no way to lock up.

She told me Vick was hoping I'd weigh in, join the team. The look in her eye(s) said she had some doubts.

Looking from her to him, I said, "Just came this close to getting my . . . how about you give me a day or so."

She told me to take my time, meantime they'd be working on a slogan. "Something like, 'Maxx, it's got X appeal.'" Looking at me for my reaction, she gave a head shake, her do looking like it might topple.

"Yeah, that could work." I looked around for where I parked my wreck.

Vick saying this deal might top his cardboard furniture deal, how he was negotiating with a good Elvis, guy we knew from the Don.

"Elvis in the Don?"

"You remember Archie Roehall."

"Sure, I remember Arch, but . . ."

"Man's gone Elvis now." Vick said he was hoping to get him onboard for the Health & Wellness Trade Show down at the Ex. "Just picture the King endorsing something like this, hair shining and all combed back, the sideburns."

"Archie, huh?" Elvis from the Don Jail.

"Okay, maybe we're not talking the best Elvis," he said, "just one we can afford, for now anyway."

Jackie saying, "I mean, who's got better hair than Elvis, right?" Shaking her head again.

"Hard to argue."

"Anyway, Maxx takes off, we're gonna put an Elvis in every major trade show, right across the board," he said.

"Like shopping-mall Santas," I said, the only one smiling. Fishing for my keys, I took the round one and unlocked the Valiant's door, thanking them again for showing up, promising I'd think it over, the least I could do. Sticking in the ignition key, I shut the door. In need of another drink, I considered where I could pick up a box of wine at this hour.

The lights were off at *Deli*-cious, the sign out front promising meatloaf for tomorrow's special. Came with a Coke and a side of dills. Only four bucks. Reminded me I hadn't had dinner yet.

No grey van as I turned at Annette. I switched the radio on. The commentator was talking about another gang shooting in Rexdale, saying it was getting worse than Scarborough, which he called Scarlem. No mention of the AutoPark car lot getting shot up. Guessing you needed a body count these days to make the local news.

Leaning the fireplace poker against the wall, I closed the door and made the call from the bedroom office, giving Ted the short strokes. The creaking floorboard meant Ann was listening from the hall. Ted making it easy, inviting me out on his boat, seeing tomorrow was my day off.

Hanging up, I pulled the door open, Ann smiling at the threshold, wrapped in her pink housecoat, the classifieds tucked under her arm. "Have enough to eat?"

"Yeah, pork chops were fine. Do them just right."

Ann asking about my day.

"Sold a Buick Electra, fully loaded."

She asked how much, and I told her what I made on it, then told her we were set to ship more cars up from Poughkeepsie, the reason for the call to Ted.

"Uh huh." Flapping the Globe to the classifieds, she pointed to a job ad circled in red. "Place called PlanIt, looking for a management exec. Says salary plus benefits."

"I got a job, Ann."

"Can't hurt to call, right?"

I gave her the look, feeling tired.

"We got bills, Jeff, you know, going from overdue to yellow."

"Ad say they hire ex-cons?"

She put her hand to her hip, saying, "There're places give second chances."

"Look, I'll talk to Ted, ask about a draw, how's that?"

"Talk when?"

"Tomorrow soon enough?" Told her we were having a strategy meeting out on his boat.

She snugged up the housecoat, her eyes flashed, her lips tightening.

"Look, told you how this works, Ann. Need some time to make it work."

Tapping a finger on the ad, she said, "PlanIt offers a company car."

"Matter of fact, Ted told me to pick one off the lot."

"Yeah, when's that?"

"All in time, plus we already got a car."

"One you're running in the ground. Way you're heading, your job's going to cost us money, money we don't have."

"Okay, said I'll talk to Ted."

Turning, she said she was going to bed, had an early shift.

"Doing my best here, Ann."

Stopping, she gave me another kind of look and told me to catch a shower, wash the day off.

I knew the look. Returning the fireplace poker to the living room, I put my mug in the old Norge and grabbed a towel from the linen closet.

Following me in, she sat on the toilet while I got the water temperature right, peeled off my clothes, dropped them in a heap on the mat.

"Remember that place I told you about, one with the blue shutters?"

"Over by Baby Point or someplace, yeah," I said, stepping under the spray.

"Been on the market a while now," she said, louder so I could hear, calling it a fix-me-upper with potential, reminding me it had three bedrooms, a swing set in the yard.

She was back at it, thinking about kids, filling up the bedrooms, seeing them on the swing set.

Fresh out of the Don and feeling my age, I was having a hard time picturing myself pushing a kid on a swing. Turning up the hot water, pretty sure I read somewhere the heat killed sperm cells without affecting the urge. Before getting out, I turned it all the way to cold and tried to kill that, too.

Easing the thirty-six-footer from its slip, Ted tugged the Jays cap low, blocking the slant of the early sun coming across the Scarborough horizon. Bluffers Park was row after row of masts. Maneuvering his Sea Ray along the inner channel, Ted stayed to starboard of a line of scullers, kept his wake down, hearing me tell about the guys with the pruners and the Nena, how Vick walked in with the cockeyed woman, saving my ass. Said Vick suggested a gun.

"Man's right about that. Got to asshole-proof yourself," Ted said, reaching into the map pocket for a Ruger, saying, "Stick it in your pocket."

Hefting it, I guessed the kind of time an ex-con got just for holding one.

"Better you than them, right?"

Grabbing the rail, I kept from doing the staggering two-step, Ted angling into the light chop coming from the south. It was my first time off terra firma, breathing in the lake air, looking at the chalk grey of the bluffs.

"Good he came along when he did," Ted said, then complained about Vick's never-ending memos. "Guy can sell, don't get me wrong, but he's got no focus. And what's with this hair crap?"

"A little side action." I shrugged.

"Fucking embarrassing. And leaving memos around the showroom about Elvis fucking Christ. Come on, man, give me a break."

That got me laughing.

"Tell you, one more fuckin' memo, I swear, I'll chop his fingers myself, save Mal Rocca the trouble."

Both of us laughing.

"Read the one he sent last night?" he said.

I shook my head.

"Memo said he wants to put an Elvis in every trade show," he said, shaking his head and giving more throttle, the engine rumbling and kicking like a thoroughbred — nearly pitched me into the aft seat.

"Love it out here," he said, "the breeze, away from the bullshit. See anything coming at you a mile away."

Tucking the Ruger in my jacket, liking the feel of it, eyes on a gull diving and coming up with a baitfish, shaking its head and swallowing the silver body, then flapping its wings on the water and taking off.

"Been watching you, think you're up for running the show, here and maybe Poughkeepsie, too."

"Yeah?"

Easing on the throttle, Ted let her plane out.

"Yeah, no doubt I'm up for it, but how about the part you haven't been talking about?"

"Time's coming for that." He looked at me, saying, "Squaring up some debts, like I told you, getting things worked out." Reaching in his jacket again, he took an envelope and held it out.

"What's this?"

"Call it walking-round money."

Opening it, I fingered the bills, forgetting the part he wasn't talking about. Counting out twenty-five hundred bucks. Man, I felt like firing a round across the water.

Throttling down, he grinned at me and waved at a sailboat coming abreast of the Sea Ray. Reaching a bottle of Pirate's Choice from under the console, he told me there were glasses in the galley.

Going below, I hunted through a cupboard and came back as the forty-footer slid past. Two oiled beauties laid out on towels, tan and ripe as fruit, smiling over at us. An old boy at the tiller, his white captain's cap tipped low on his head. Money, hell, I could just about taste it. Waving at the women, them waving back.

Ted slowed enough to fill the plastic glasses, the sun sparkling on the water, the sea breeze, a gentle lap of waves against the hull, the two of us working on that nice rum buzz. With a pistol and two grand in my pocket, just a few weeks out of hell, I was feeling more than the rum; I was feeling the hundred-and-thirty-pound monkey climbing off my back, guessing Ann's weight. Betting she'd drop that pink housecoat and screw me silly tonight.

Randy Hooper tossed another roll of cash on the desk, Vick's basement office. Vick sitting in his swivel chair, Randy standing, bending and taking Vick's dog from under the desk, the top of his head nearly touching the low ceiling.

"Name?" Randy said.

"What?"

"Dog's got a name, right?"

"Tina." Vick looked at the schnauzer in his hands. No Pony White this time. And no drill. Still, Vick felt uneasy, telling him what he found out, how Ted was putting Jeff Nichols in charge, giving him the spare office.

"Why'd I give a shit about that?"

"Maybe better to talk to him than me, is all."

"Already talking to you." Randy patted the dog, waiting.

Vick telling him there should be more cars coming from Poughkeepsie in the next couple of days. Guessing Mateo would have his guys strap Uzis under the rides, something to keep the Bent Boys from blasting up the AutoPark again.

"Guessing's worth shit," Randy said, setting the dog in

Vick's lap, putting a hand on the chair, tipping it back and leaning close. "Want to know exactly when and where."

"Yeah, sure. Do what I can."

Randy patted the dog again, saying, "Maybe I better meet this Jeff."

"Yeah, yeah, sure." Vick saying he'd set it up.

"Nice meeting you, Tina." Turning, Randy went up the stairs, left Vick sitting at his desk, cradling the schnauzer.

. . . POINT MAN

The usual midday buzz in *Deli*-cious. Voices rose over the clatter of dishes, the smell of cooking oil coming from the fryer. Business types washed down daily specials with dark roast, the busboy juggled a stack of dishes, angling past the waitress with her arms loaded with plates, weaving through the tables.

We sat at the same booth by the window. The woman behind me was embalmed in eau-de-cheap, the scent twisting the taste of my corned beef, a two-inch pile of heartburn on rye. Ted was talking shop around a mouthful of clubhouse, asking how I'd fare crossing the border, on account of doing time.

"Just got to show my driver's license, far's I know." Looking out the window, I caught the same grey Econoline rolling down the street, pointed to it.

"Guys tried to circumcise you, huh?"

"Sending their message."

"Gave you the .32, right? Send your own message."

"Letting me know they're still around," I said, watching the van drive off.

"Gonna square things with Mal Rocca next day or so, and this shit goes away." Ted looked at his sandwich, biting at a strip of bacon hanging past the toasted bread. He told me selling cars would be slow till the workmen were out of there. He wanted me making a run down to Poughkeepsie, meet his man Mateo Cruz and get a look at the operation.

"Yeah?"

"Said you wanted to know the whole deal, right?"

"Yeah."

"Meantime . . ." Ted reached in his jacket and pulled out a small cardboard box, something he had Bonnie order up before she walked out on him. A business card taped on top: the company logo and my name and the word manager under it. The address and phone number centered below that.

"Impresses the chicks," Ted said, smiling and biting into his sandwich.

Rubbing a thumb across the embossed type, I said thanks, taking another glance out the window.

"Forget those van guys," Ted said.

"Not that." I told him it was time to go feed the meter, pointing to the Valiant parked across the street.

"That's your ride, huh?"

"'Fraid so."

"Don't get me wrong, Jeff, but rust's got a way of unsettling the tire kickers. Need something sharp, something that leaves an impression."

"Guess she got old while I was inside."

He watched me run out to the old wreck and feed quarters in the meter, saying when I got back, "Forget waiting on the next shipment. Take one off the floor."

"Company car?"

"Call it what you want. Pick one didn't get shot up too bad. One'll get you down to Poughkeepsie and back, looking like you're in the game."

Thanking him, I tried to picture which one hadn't been shot up too bad. Getting that feeling that things were still looking up in spite of the showroom getting shot up: office, gun, money, car. Couldn't wait to tell Ann.

The waitress swung by with the coffee pot, topping up our cups, asking if we wanted pie. Watching her go, Ted said he wouldn't mind a piece of that pie, taking a card from the box, feeling in his jacket for a pen that wasn't there. I handed him mine. Marcel's Barber Shop stamped down the barrel, done like a red-and-white barber's pole. The phone number in black under the logo.

Ted smiled, seeing the pen was from Marcel's, saying as he wrote, "Go see my man, Walter. Fix you up with a nice suit, something sharp."

"A suit, huh?"

"Say you're with me, and he sets up an account. Can pay it off like an installment plan." Ted waving a hand like that was that, looking back out the window. "Fast lane's coming up, my boy. Time to put some distance between you and the guys with green stuff between their teeth, know what I mean?" Clapping my shoulder as the waitress came back. She told him he had another call, pointing to the wall phone, said it sounded urgent.

"Getting so's a man can't eat," Ted said, taking his wallet and dropping another five on the table, told her he wasn't here. The waitress taking it and giving a weak smile, moving on, looking like she wanted to clout him with the coffee pot.

"Come on, let's go," he said.

"I get my pen back?"

Ted looked at the pen still in his hand, passed it to me, shaking his head, going for the door.

. . . PIECE OF THE PIE

Had my eye on an Audi Quattro in Zermatt silver, mainly because it was German, but it had been shot up too bad in the drive-by, the engine block cracked and the oil pan bleeding, the body pocked with holes, tufts of upholstery sticking from the Kodiak leather. The Gran Fury was an '82, an M-body Plymouth with the salon trim and a Slant-6. Nothing special about it: Baron-red paint and whitewalls the only things that kept her from looking like a cop car. Still, it beat my old Valiant, which I parked around the side next to the dumpster. Got in the Gran Fury, playing with the buttons for the AM/FM with CB and Dolby, CHUM FM playing some April Wine. "I Like To Rock" rattling through the door speakers.

Slipping on my shades, I shifted the three-speed and rolled out, stopping for the first light along Annette, getting the feel.

A leggy blonde of the first order crossed at the next light. High breasts and white teeth. Long legs in heels. Nothing about the Gran Fury made her look over. Still, I was feeling my days of bum deals and scratching a living were over.

The blonde walked on, and I drove by, April Wine fading out and giving way to Boz Scaggs, singing about putting the money down and letting it roll.

Ann stood in her usual spot, her arms wrapped around herself, leaning against the library wall, keeping out of the wind. Looking right past me.

I tapped the horn, peeling off the shades. Everyone but Ann looking over. Pressing the button for the power window, I lowered it and called, "Hey, baby, need a lift?"

She took a double look, saying, "Oh, my God . . ."

I told her to get in.

"How'd you . . ." I could see she was thinking grand theft auto, her eyes big as plates, mouth hanging open. Climbing in, she slid her hand over the buttoned-down leatherette. Pressing another button, I hoped to heat her side of the split-bench seat.

"You lose your mind? I mean, tell me you didn't . . ."

"What, steal it?"

"Was thinking lease it, but please, just tell me."

"Perks of the job, Ann. You wanted me to ask, I asked. Ted told me to take my pick."

"And this was it?"

Easing from the curb, I let that go, checking my mirrors, telling her about the day out on Ted's yacht, what it felt like on the lake, then, "Really thought I jacked this, huh?"

"Maybe for a second." Wiggling in the seat, Ann was feeling the heat. Only ever sat herself on cheap vinyl before. A smile on her face.

Taking a business card from my pocket, I held it out between two fingers.

"What's this?" She looked at it.

I pointed to where it said manager. "Stepping up, Ann, like I told you." Letting it sink in, I reached past her, taking the envelope from the glovebox, wagging it — the pistol under the ownership manual and street map. Loved watching her mouth drop open, a bit of a strangled cry coming out.

"Oh, my God . . ." Rubbing the bills between her fingers. Looking at me wide-eyed, like maybe it was a dream.

"What'd I tell you, huh?"

A hand to her chest, the other rifling the bills, Ann counted, then recounted.

I slipped my shades back on, both hands on the wheel, the Slant-6 purring, maybe knocking a bit, but I didn't care. This was the best day of my life.

Leaning across the split-seat, she turned my head and kissed me, long and hard, said she was loving the heat on the seat, wiggling like a hen on a nest.

I said maybe we should take this baby through the car wash, Ann grinning, getting my meaning, said for what she had in mind we were going to need more than two minutes.

"What say we take a spin by Baby Point, find that place you were talking about, one with the blue shutters?"

"Oh, come on. Just get me home," Ann said, laughing. "Got to fix supper."

"Uh uhn, not tonight." Telling her I made reservations at the Old Mill, a table for two.

"We can't just . . ."

"Tonight, it's you, me and a bottle of whatever comes with a cork." Nodding at the cash in her hand.

Thinking about it, she couldn't come up with a reason not to, counting it again. "God, we're moving up." Putting a hand on my thigh, she half hummed, half sang what she remembered of the Jeffersons theme, getting her turn at bat, finally getting that piece of the pie.

A couple of wrong turns before I pulled up to the Re/Max sign. The two of us taking the property in. Ann drinking in the green craftsman with blue shutters, a yard for the kids to play.

The place looked deserted to me, the lawn overgrown, weeds in the flower beds, a sway to the roofline, a chimney in need of pointing, one of the upstairs windows boarded. The place was lot-value only, but this was Baby Point, at least close enough to call it that and smell the stinking rich.

Tucking the envelope away, her fingers brushed the Ruger in the glovebox. Moving the map, she looked at it, saying, "What on Earth . . ."

"Guess it's Ted's." I clapped the glovebox shut.

"And what's he doing with it?"

"I don't know, the guy's American."

She frowned.

"That or, maybe came with the car. It's American, too, right?"

"Funny man."

I pointed to the fountain, then wrote the Re/Max number on the back of one of the cards, said I'd get us a showing.

Ann saying we could never afford it, wiggling on the leatherette. "Still, nice to dream."

"Told you I'll make it happen, right?" Coaxing the Gran Fury to make a three-point turn, I headed for the Old Mill. Ann watching me, still not believing it.

First time a valet got my door, calling me sir and taking my keys. Last time somebody got my door was when the security patrol cuffed me after the bottle I set on the roof and forgot rolled and smashed from the ride I was jacking. I tipped the valet a deuce.

It was happening. The feel of success going through me like a current. Going around and holding Ann's door, the two of us heading inside to the hostess desk. I told her I had reservations, gave her my name. Calling me sir, she smiled and led us to a table. The two of us taking in the vaulted ceiling, the thick beams and chandeliers.

Yeah, I'd go see Ted's tailor, thinking navy with pin-stripes, a couple white shirts and ties, guessing I'd get used to them, learn to wrap a Windsor knot, wondering if cuffs and pleats were still in. Taking the leather-bound wine list from the waiter, I scanned it like I knew what I was doing and ordered up a bottle, guessed at those prices they all came with a cork.

. . . THE BIG E

The news anchor on the Q was going on about the city's escalating gang violence: "Police are calling last night's gun battle retaliation for the shooting death of Dustin Bent outside Hamilton's Westdale Regent." Naming the two Dreads gunned down outside a tenement last night, one cashing in en route to Etobicoke General, the second in intensive care. Saying, "Metro police are talking to witnesses and looking into leads."

Couldn't find a spot on Strachan, so I parked on Wellington, leaving the pistol under the seat, getting out and scanning the street, a stench coming from the meat-packing plant past the rail yard. A transport passed, snouts and ears poking through the slats. Remembered somebody calling the place Hogtown.

Faded red swirls, the white long ago turned to yellow, the barber pole spun in its bug-filled acrylic cylinder, a relic from the sixties. The signboard declared the place was Marcel's. Haircuts five bucks, any style you want.

Vick was sitting close to the door with a dog-eared Cosmopolitan, one leg crossing the other, looking up as

I came in. Next to him sat Archie Roehall, looking like a morning-after Elvis, one who was suffering from a rhinestoned night. Eyes red-rimmed and bloodshot. Hair and sideburns in need of a lube and comb. Flip-flops on his feet, toenails in need of a trim. No sequined splendor about this guy. Just an Elvis they could afford, like Vick said.

A woman sat across from them, looked to be taking her mid-forties on the chin, glancing over with an obvious devotion for the King. Her youngest sat next to her, the kid about six; his forefinger was excavating a nostril, had it jammed up to the first knuckle. The pop-bottle lenses were crooked on account of the boring, gave the kid an owlish look which he aimed at me.

Peeling off the shades, I stepped to Vick, nodding over at Marcel, the man with one of those trimmers in his fat hand, buzzing away at the older kid's head. The one with the pop-bottle eyes kept the finger twisting in his nose, looking at me.

"You remember Archie?" Vick said.

I said sure I did.

Getting up, he recaptured a flip-flop with his toes, offering a damp palm at the end of a loose wrist, clearing his throat, looked like he was looking for a place to spit.

We talked some small change for a minute, this guy looking a long way from the guy I knew in the orange jumpsuit. "You looking good, Jeff."

"Yeah, you too. Different, I mean . . . Elvis, huh?"

"Yeah, it's a living, you know." Running a hand along a sideburn.

"Man's being modest," Vick said, getting up and slinging

an arm around his man's shoulder — maybe he was holding him up — looking at me, saying, "Archie's gonna blow the roof off the trade show."

"That right, huh?"

"In case we got a doubter here, Arch, how about you give him a taste?"

"What, here?" Archie looking around, Marcel looking over, kept working on the kid's hair, the mother saying she wished Archie would, clasping her hands together.

"What the hell." Taking a breath and steadying himself, Archie gave a pelvic shake and dished up some a cappella Oh baby, let me be your teddy bear.

The mother gasped, and I had to admit the guy was pretty good; Marcel kept on buzzing hair, looking sour.

"Hey, come on now, give us a bit more than that," Vick said. The mother nodding, hands still together.

"How about you, Jeff, you got a favorite?" Archie said.

"I don't know . . . 'Devil in Disguise,' maybe 'Return to Sender,' both pretty good."

Archie was hitting his stride now, winked at the mother, saying, "How about you, doll?"

She practically whinnied, put fingers to her throat, just a whisper coming out, "Love Me Tender."

Singing about some love, tender and sweet, Archie did the old tune justice, tipping his chin down, rocking his hips, hit her with a baritone low G, the magazine slipping from her fingers.

The older boy saying, "Mom?"

Flicking her hand at him, she straightened, said she was just fine.

Smiling at me, Vick said, "Hell man, we're gonna make a killing. Ought to hear this cat do his Aloha set."

"Thought we were going with the Vegas?" Archie looked at him, serious.

"Hey, you're the King, right?" Vick said, grinning, shooting him a play elbow. Saying to me, "You got to get in on this, man."

"Why you called me down here, to say hi, hear Archie singing?" No offense to Archie, I said, but I was getting tired of the flip-flop show.

"Got something else." Vick walked me to the door, saying, "Got this other guy I want you to meet." Telling me Randy Hooper was ripe to drop some money on the hair deal, and Vick wanted to know how I'd handle something like that. Help him out for old times' sake.

Thinking we could have done it over the phone, I turned to the pop-bottle kid, the kid's finger still doing the nostril twist. Staring at me.

"Tell you what, how about you swing by for a barbie?" Vick said.

"Barbie?"

"Barbecue."

"The hair thing, huh?"

"Little this, little that, but don't overthink it, man," Vick said, "but so you know, Marcel's on his second case of the stuff, less than a month."

I looked at Marcel, the old man shrugging, finished buzzing the older kid's head.

"Just pop over, hear Randy out," Vick said. "Tell you,

man, after the trade show, this thing's going through the top. Promise you that."

Pulling the cloth away like an artistic reveal, Marcel brushed hair from the kid's shoulders, the kid leaping from the chair and bolting over to his mother and punching his brother on the arm. Coke-bottle eyes lashed back with a Nike, the mother getting between them, swiping at the finger in the nose, dragging the younger kid to Marcel's chair. The kid hooking a foot around the side table stacked with magazines, not making it easy.

Marcel took the reprieve, the mother needing a couple of minutes of strong-arming to get the kid into the chair. My guess, this happened every time they came in.

"Need a trim?" Marcel said to me, saying he heard the showroom got shot to shit.

"Yeah, you should see it." Ran a hand over my head and said I was fine.

"You want to bail on the AutoPark, I understand. No sweat finding you something else."

"Guess I'll hang in, see how it plays out," I said.

"No shit," Vick said, "Ted giving you an office, making you the man." Marcel and I looking at him, Vick waving it off, saying to Marcel, "Tell him what you said about Maxx."

"Said it smells," Marcel said, giving him an annoyed look.

"That's the smell of money, my friend," Vick said, play-punching Marcel's arm. "The shit works, you'll see."

Looking like he wanted to counterpunch, Marcel looked at Archie, asked him, "How about you, you want a trim?" Getting a no, he turned back to me, saying, "Like I said, you want out, give me a call." Then he went back for his barber's chair.

The pop-bottle kid caught some leverage, the mother locking on something looking like a judo move. Marcel catching the kid from falling, slinging him back into the chair, draping the cloth around his neck, snugging it, maybe it looked a little too tight.

"Shooting an infomercial later," Vick said to me. "Want to tag along, Jackie'll be there. Meet Truman, our video guy. Grab a couple brew."

I told him I had shit to do, reaching the doorknob, thinking I just wasted half the morning, looking back at Marcel pinning the kid in the chair. Thinking life's gonna kick that kid to the curb.

Looking up and down Wellington, I figured since I was down this end of town, I'd swing over to Spadina and drop in on Ted's tailor, get measured up for a suit. Start looking the part, get away from the guys with green shit in their teeth.

. . . DRESSING TO THE RIGHT

Price-bound shopping and overstocks, ends-of-lines and closing sales. All of that was in my past. I was feeling like a winner, my arm being raised by Walter the tailor.

Taking in my build, Walter eyeballed one shoulder then the other. The furrow across his forehead deepened. Old and grey with a stoop, Walter took his work serious. Calling me Ted Bracey's man, Walter wondered what happened to the last one working at the AutoPark, the one named Robbie. Never came back for his extra pants, grey in a nice tweed.

"Man wasn't cut out for it," I said, told him he quit.

He dropped my arm and gave a sigh, picking up his chart.

"Something wrong?"

"God makes mistakes and Walter fixes." He wrote something.

The bell over the door chimed and the two guys from the van walked in, Egg and Bundy. Had me looking for a back way out, my windbreaker hanging on the rack, in easy reach, the Ruger in the pocket.

A beat-to-hell Expos ball cap on his head, Bundy wasn't looking the type to walk into a tailor shop, smiling and coming up the center aisle. Egg stayed at the front by a table of bolts, looking at the fabric.

Saying he'd be right with them, Walter told me he wanted to add a little padding, even up the shoulders.

"Whatever you think," I said, then to Bundy, "You mutts not getting the message, huh?"

Bundy said, "Don't like the way we left things hanging."

I nodded, telling Walter we were done for now, reaching for my windbreaker.

Slinging the tape over his shoulder, Walter went to his counter, muttering something, picking up the ringing phone by the cash, answering and holding it out to me, rolling his eyes, saying, "It's for you."

With the windbreaker under an arm, I took the phone from him, kept my eyes on Bundy and said, "Yeah?"

Checking his notes, Walter ran the tape from my waistband, asking which way I dressed.

"How's Saturday, say around two?" Vick said on the phone.

"Gonna waste more of my time, huh?"

Walter finding the answer by hand.

"Hey, hey," I twisted away. "Fuck's next, a cavity search?"

Walter jotting a note on his chart.

"You're on speaker by the way," Vick said.

"Look, Vick, kinda busy . . ."

"Like he's doing us a favor," Jackie's voice, sounding from across the room.

"Who's that, Jackie?"

"Of course, it's me," the woman sounding annoyed.

Said I'd try to make it, and I hung up and started for the door.

Blocking the exit, Egg put his hands wide to stop me. I showed the butt of the pistol and told him to give me the keys to his van, keeping one eye on Bundy.

Looking at the pistol, Egg thought about his chances, then fumbled in his pocket.

Taking his keys, I went out the door, the bell chiming. I was halfway across Spadina when they stepped out behind me. Bundy and Egg stood watching as I walked to the Gran Fury. Walter threw the lock and turned the sign in the window from open to closed.

Tossing Egg's keys at a sewer grate, I heard them splash below. Giving a salute, I got in and pulled away, knowing I just swatted the hive.

. . . COMMON GROUND

Whatever the hell was coating my tongue looked like curd, as yellow as Jackie's teeth. My head throbbed, part of the usual morning fuzz. Drinking wine like I was making up for lost time. Looking at my reflection, I told myself to ease up on the stuff. Washing my hands, I stuck them under the blow-dryer. Closing the men's room door, I walked between a couple of Chevys on the showroom floor. Vick was working a pair of college kids standing next to the one with the stripes and wide Firestones. A crew was installing the new plate-glass windows, their truck parked out front, glass racks down both sides. Going up to my office, I shut the door, taking the Ruger from under my jacket and tossing it in the drawer behind the Cohibas.

Leaning back in the chair, I tried to get my mind off the two guys dogging me and onto the place with the blue shutters. Doing that Zen breathing Ann tried to teach me, taking in the calming bubbling of the desk fountain. None of it working, my mind swung to sex, that part of my life doing alright, then I was thinking about money. Still had seventy-five hundred from my grand theft auto days, money stashed behind the heat register in the spare room, money Ann didn't know about. Had more stashed in an old can of Behr's stain, back of the garage. That plus the twenty-five hundred Ted handed me, I'd be close to the downstroke on the house. Staring at the fountain, I got to thinking the guns had to be hidden on the cars being detailed. Way I figured it, they were taken out up here, probably at Ted's Quickie Wash.

The tap at the door had me jumping, Vick coming in, tossing paperwork on the desk, parking himself in the spare chair. "Got these kids thinking they got me a nickel under sticker."

"Yeah." I spun the papers around and had a look, Ted wanting me to sign off on all the deals from here on.

"Gonna tell them I got another guy chomping at the bit, get the little shits outbidding themselves."

Stroking out the price, I asked what he wanted and scribbled in the new number, initialing it, saying, "They go for it, toss in the free wash for a year bit."

"Screw 'em, these guys are rubes. Lucky I let them drive off with a full tank."

"You're all heart." I slid the papers back.

"So when's Ted gonna give us the full picture, you figure?" he said.

I gave a shrug.

Picking up the papers, he said he had another couple coming back for a second kick at the Country Squire of their dreams, the bullet holes all patched up and new woodgrain vinyl down the sides. Vick pointed above my head at the Chuvalo poster, asking, "You ever see the champ fight?"

"Everybody's asking me that."

"Saw him a couple times, hell of a chin. Fought Ali twice."

"Yeah, heard that. He win?"

"Not the point," Vick said, then asked, "So, when we getting more cars coming? Way I'm going, gonna sell out."

"Ted's auction guy picked up like a dozen more. Being detailed now."

Vick pulled out his smokes, found his box of wooden matches, saying, "Let me know when, huh?" Taking my pen, he scratched out the counter price I wrote, scribbled in a new number, took the paperwork and turned for the door. Lighting up, saying, "Rubes are gonna pay for my night out."

"Yeah, with Jackie?"

"You kidding? Had a thing back in the day, but the woman's not really my kind."

"What kind's that?"

"Kind with Randy, guy you're gonna meet Saturday." Vick winked and tossed the match in the Zen fountain, leaving the door open, taking the steps. I could hear him telling the guys waiting he had good news.

. . . WHAT IF?

The Re/Max sign had fallen over on the lawn. A Mercedes sedan sat in the driveway. I rolled the Gran Fury to the curb.

Switching off the news, Ann said she was getting tired of these gang wars, wondering what was happening to this town, used to be a safe place to raise kids, then, "Oh, so excited I nearly forgot," telling me Ted's wife, Liz, called this morning, inviting us to Ted's sixtieth.

"Liz, huh?"

"What she said."

"And you're telling me now?"

"On account of the excitement." She said it was going to be at some new place over on Dupont, couldn't think of the name right then. "Anyway, I wrote it down. Let me enjoy this, will you?"

I shut off the engine, both of us taking the place in for the second time, Ann pointing out the potential, the flower boxes, room on the porch for a rocker. Still looked pretty run-down to me. Getting out, the best thing I could come up with, there weren't any Tibors in this price range.

Penny Mansell, the realtor, stood on the stoop, casting her realtor's eye down on us. Betting she made us for low-income types with a modest car, barely qualifying.

Hooking Ann's arm, I walked her up the drive, taking in the choke weed spilling from flower boxes, ivy clinging to the stucco. Water in the stone fountain looking green and milky with algae. A cherub with its pecker snapped off standing over it. Don't know why, but I started thinking about where it could be, the pecker. Maybe it got tossed in a shed out back, or was lying in the basement. Then wondering if it could be reattached — just didn't look right like that. What kind of a message did it send?

"Jeff?" Ann nudging me up the front steps, Penny Mansell waiting with a smile and moist handshake, sprayed dye job and red lipstick across her mouth. Working the lockbox hooked on the wrought-iron rail, she made small talk, getting the key and shouldering open the door, asking if we had kids. Ann saying that was a work in progress. Penny throwing in it was a great neighborhood for families, a fenced yard, a school a block away, walking distance to the IGA. Telling us the owners had just reduced the asking price, getting lots of calls now. "Not much in this price range, not around here."

Stepping into the front hall, Penny's heels clicked on creaking floorboards. She went in search of light switches. Ann was turning around, drinking it in, mentally placing the furniture. I went around checking for wood-rot, noting a tea-stained watermark on the ceiling.

Shoving up one of the casement windows, Penny asked, "So, you folks been looking long?"

"Kicked a few tires," I said and went to the other window, pushing at it, banging the sash with my palm.

"You a handy guy, Jeff?"

"Not so you'd notice."

Leaning past me, Penny flipped the casement latch, sliding up the window, doing it with a smile. "There we go." Excusing herself, she went to the kitchen, said she had to make a call, leaving us to look around.

Ann stood beaming, never seen her look like that, asking what I thought.

"Well, needs work, but —"

"Just a coat of paint, freshen it right up." Taking my hand, she squeezed, went to the built-in cabinets, saying there was room for a nice set of china, china we didn't have. And space for the Feng Shui fountain on top.

I went, kneeled down and fiddled with the fireplace damper, got a pile of soot coming down. Clapping it from my hands.

Calling from the kitchen, Penny said there was room for an extra bedroom in the basement. Then went back to her call.

"Place'll be as big as Deb's," Ann said, watching me clap my hands.

Calling to Penny, I asked why it's been empty so long.

"Estate sale. One son wants to sell. Other one . . . well, grew up here . . . guess it's hard to let go of." Then she went back to her call.

"We'd never qualify," Ann whispered.

Not sure why, but I said I'd take care of it with the bank. Looking for somewhere to wipe my hands.

"What're you going to do, mortgage at gunpoint?"

"Gonna make it happen, Ann, that's what."

Coming back from the kitchen, Penny said the sellers would take back a second, noting my blackened hands, telling me the sink in the kitchen should be working.

After I washed up and finger-flicked my hands dry, we went up the groaning staircase and took in the bedrooms, the bathroom with a stained tub. Ann loving the his-and-her closets, doing that Vanna White thing with her hands, pointing things out, saying we could be happy here. I had to admit, in spite of the work it needed, the place had potential. Her look telling me if Penny hadn't been there, she would have pulled me down on the creaking hardwood and chris-tened the place, right then and there, getting herself in that family way. Looking out the window, Penny pointed out the rusting swing set in the yard.

. . . MOVING MONEY

A nice view of the lake from the living room, leaded glass window. Leaning back on the overstuffed sofa, a fern on either side, Mal Rocca folded his thick arms, looking at Ted Bracey over his glasses. His hired muscle, Cully, stood by the brick fireplace, a big guy in a tight T-shirt, looking at Ted like here was another douchebag about to plead for more time. Cully looking like he was half bored, half enjoying this.

Putting a foot up on his knee, a two-tone brogue with no sock, Mal considered him, saying, "Better not be playing me." Calling him Teddy.

"You made your point, Mal. And like I told you, something came up. Anyway, got it right here."

"Extra points, too?"

"All of it." Tapping his fingers on the briefcase, Ted nodded and set it on the glass coffee table, careful not to scrape the polished surface. Flipping the latches, he turned it enough to show the stacks of hundreds inside. Cully craned his thick neck close for a look and grunted. Taking a double fistful of stacks, Ted set them on the glass, reached for more and fired a shot through the case. The first bullet took Cully in the hip and sent him reeling. Catching himself on the mantel, he wailed. Pulling out the suppressed Ruger, Ted fired again, putting one through Cully's chest, the man thrown down, blood splattering the fireplace. Then he turned to Mal. Mal with his brogues on the carpet now, bug-eyed, hands up in surrender.

"See, not playing at all, Mal," Ted said as he fired, caught Mal in the side of the throat. Mal knocking the planter next to him over. Clapping a hand to his neck, Mal tipped to the floor, mouth open, gagging sound coming out. "Here's your extra points, asshole." Ted emptied the clip in Mal's gut. Dropping the Ruger back in the case, shoving the stacks back on top, Ted latched it and walked out of there, cool as you please, the side of the case with the bullet hole turned toward his leg. He walked to where he parked on the next street, one below Queen, smelling alewives from down on the beach, thinking the city ought to do something about that.

Creases like craters on Mother Hibbit's forehead, grey threading through her hair, the woman calling it frosty. Ann's sister, Debra Ryan, on the other hand, was doing a commendable job mocking Old Man Time. I bet on a face-lift and a good bit of augmentation under the sweater, not the first things about her that ever struck me as false, never getting past her detestable nature. Giving out ritual hugs that barely touched, I made the smiles look real, remembered my promise to Ann to play nice.

Trudging up the stoop, Dennis puffed like the twin Vuittons were packed with cinder blocks, the cabbie backing down the drive of our rental dump, frowning at what I bet was the lousy tip he just got. Setting the bags down, two totes sliding from his shoulders, Dennis pecked Ann's cheek. Giving me a surprised look, like maybe I just teleported in, shaking my hand as he glanced around, saying, "So, this is it, huh?"

"Afraid so," Ann said.

Dennis Jr. raced up the steps, looking more like Debra than Dennis, exploding past the adult legs, flying a toy plane. Hooked left into the living room, not letting the mismatched furniture restrict his movement, getting good height as he bounced across the sofa cushions, the kid right at home, making rat-a-tat-tat sounds, blond hair flying.

"He's gotten so . . . big," Ann said, trading smiles with me, her eyes pleading.

"He'll land in a few minutes," Debra said, looking from Ann to me. "Kid's been cooped all day, needs to let loose, you know how it is."

"Should've seen you at his age," Mother Hibbit said, the woman crossing herself and Debra rolling her eyes.

"Well, come on in . . . just leave the luggage." Ann hooked Dennis's arm, ushering him into the living room, delegating me to take care of the drinks.

"Black tea with a pinch of lemon will do me fine," Debra said, without looking at me.

Mother asking for a dry martini, three olives, not two, on account of it being bad luck to go with two. Dennis calling for a bourbon neat. I went in the kitchen. It was burgundy from a box or Rolling Rock, eighteen cans for the price of twelve; that, or they could all go get stuffed. Telling myself to play nice.

Filling a wine glass and grabbing a cold one, I set the glass in front of Mother, handing Dennis the can of beer. Then I stood by the kitchen threshold, waiting for the kettle to whistle.

"Hear you're working now, Jeff," Debra said, batting her eyes like something had fallen into them.

"That's right." I smiled, watching Dennis Jr. fly his plane for the stairs. Reminding myself if I could take jail, I could take three days of this, watching Debra pass Ann a gift bag. Ann looking inside, feigning delight.

"Just a little something from Alaska," Debra said.

"Oh my." Ann pulled out a pair of dolls on plastic stands, fit in the palm of her hand, crafted with the artistic skill of a twitching junkie.

"They're Yupik dolls," Debra said, "made by Yupik Eskimos."

Ann smiled, looking at me like she was hoping for rescue.

"Legend says they bring fertility and fish," Debra said.

"Come in handy around here," I said.

The kettle called, and I went about fixing Debra's tea, dunking a bag, wishing Tetley came in hemlock. Bringing in the mug, I set it down and watched Ann position the dolls on the mantel, next to the family photo: Debra, Ann, Mother Hibbit, an assortment of aunts and uncles I never met, some gone to their maker now, all of them looking grim as a lynch mob.

Debra swung the conversation to their cruise, Ann picking up the spilled cushions, punching them back into shape and setting them back on the chairs and sofa.

"Well, you can't go wrong with the navigator suite on the Seven Seas," Debra said. "Six stars, with the highest service-ratio. Was just dreamy, Annie, let me tell you. You two just have to go."

Tuning the woman out, I considered getting Dennis alone, sell him on the AutoPark, get him investing in the deal, betting Ted would cut a fat finder's fee for bringing in some legit cash. Mother Hibbit held up her empty glass, telling me to hit her again.

Nothing I'd like more. Smiling, I took the glass from the liver-spotted hand and headed back to the kitchen.

"May as well make it a double, dear, save you going back and forth." The old woman turned to Ann, saying, "Oh, Dennis took us out sightseeing. But, oh, the flies in Juneau chewed on me like I was a dish; but, uh, what was that fish we saw, Dennis dear, the big one?"

"A humpback, Mother," Dennis said, "and whale, not a fish."

"Huh, well, I stand corrected," Mother said, turning back to Ann. "Oh, and the scenery, dear, . . . oh, just so much of it. Nature all around."

Draining my Rolling Rock, I heard Dennis toss around some facts about humpbacks. Filling burgundy up to the lipstick smear on the rim, I brought the glass back in and set it in front of her, sure I heard something fall over down in the basement.

"Where's the kid?" I said.

Debra turned to me, ignoring the question, saying, "Second thought, be a dear, Jeff, fix us a bevvie, too." Holding up the mug, the untouched tea with the tag dangling. "Think I'll go White Russian . . . mmm . . . yes, that would be heaven."

Ann smiled at me. I nodded and turned back for the kitchen. Unclenching my fists, I was thinking I didn't have whatever the hell went into a White Russian, Debra calling to me, telling me to go light on the cream.

Dashing the mug in the sink, I took another wine glass and tapped the spigot. Dennis Jr. flew up the stairs and past me, stamping his feet down the hall, going for our bedroom.

Dennis came up from behind me, looked around like he was assessing, saying, "Whose Gran Fury in the driveway?"

"My driveway, right, Dennis?"

"Yeah, 'course, just . . ." Dennis saying he caught this bit on *60 Minutes*, that guy Morley talking about Chrysler and its plague of production problems, transmissions slipping from park to reverse, killing people.

"Think that was Ford, going from park to reverse," I said.

"Thought old Morley said Chrysler, but maybe you're right. Domestic, at any rate." Dennis held up his Rolling Rock, said, "Well, here's to luck, then." The two of us clinking cans, Dennis sipping his beer, saying, "So, things are really looking up, huh?"

"Yeah, fact, speaking of which, I been meaning to give you a heads up . . ." Looking around like somebody might be listening in.

Dennis saying he appreciated the heads up, drinking his beer as I laid out the car deal. Told him I'd let him sit with it, as I went and set Debra's wine glass in front of her, the woman going on about their next cruise, Riviera I think she said. Taking Mother's empty glass, I went back in the kitchen, selling the car deal, mentally adding the finder's fee to the money I had stashed behind the heat register and the can of stain, plus the twenty-five hundred Ted gave me.

. . . WATCHING FOR CLOVES

Water gurgled in the Feng Shui fountain on the dining room hutch. I was telling Dennis how the AutoPark bought up cars at stateside auctions and had them detailed in Poughkeepsie, then chained them on a trailer and hauled them north.

Ann told Mother Hibbit to watch for cloves in the cabbage, Debra chastising the kid, telling Junior not to eat like a little beast, wiping a napkin at his shirt, informing him that food slop wasn't a look.

Mother was saying she never put cloves in her cabbage, hated biting into the little devils, calling it *Rotkohl*, mispronouncing it. Debra saying she just splashed balsamic on hers, fried it with shallots.

"None for me, thanks," Dennis said to Ann. "Cabbage'll do me in. 'Specially on top of this." Jiggling his can of beer.

Debra said maybe Dennis should lay off the sauce, then turned to Dennis Jr., saying, "What happens when Daddy laps beer when he eats?"

Dennis Jr. doing a mouth-fart, laughing himself silly, nearly tipping from his chair.

Mother Hibbit did an open-mouthed gawk, saying, "Good heavens, Denny, the things your mother teaches you."

More mouth-farts coming from the kid, Debra saying that was enough, putting on the stern, telling the kid, "Eat your supper now, dear, and close your mouth." The kid saying how could he eat if his mouth was closed.

Tossing in his own parenting skills, Dennis told the kid to just do it, told him it tasted just like chicken.

Looking at the Cornish hen on his plate, the kid started blubbering about killing baby chickens.

"No, no, it's not a baby chicken. Oh, for heaven's sake." Debra scowled at Dennis, then went in like a surgeon, slicing up the meat on the kid's plate, saying, "Don't listen to your father. Chicken's chicken, now just eat up like a good boy."

Wiping the tears, Dennis Jr. said, "Baby chickens make me . . ." Mouth-farting, he was laughing himself silly.

Jumping in, Debra caught him from tipping backwards off the chair. I thought of the coiled rope out in the garage, the four or five Rolling Rocks allowing me to smile.

Debra reminded the kid this was his auntie's meal table, telling him to sit still and watch out for the cloves.

"What's a cloves?"

Plowing the serving spoon through the cabbage, Debra found one, showing it to him, saying, "Looks like this."

"Yuck."

Getting up for another Rolling Rock, I watched the kid straining cabbage through his teeth. His way of checking for cloves. Self-castration had to top spawning something like that. I thought of the owl-eyed kid at Marcel's barbershop, fighting his mother, not wanting his hair cut. No way I was signing up for fatherhood, not at fifty years of age. Dennis Jr. was showing a mouthful of the purple glop when I came back with the beer, one for me, one for Dennis.

"Oh, he's such a pistol," Mother Hibbit said to me, sliding me her empty glass.

I was thinking I'd be happy to get mine, the Ruger out in the glovebox.

Sliding off his chair, the kid declared he had to pee and skipped from the room.

"He okay on his own?" I said.

"Oh, sure, he's fine," Debra said. "So, Jeff, top of hawking used cars, Ann mentioned you've been out looking at houses. Getting in the hunt, are we?"

"Yeah, guess one place caught our eye." I popped the tab on the can and took a swallow of beer, glancing at Ann.

"You got a collective eye, too, huh?" Dennis said, the two of us clinking cans. Dennis grinning, catching Debra's icy stare.

"Yeah, be a nice-sized place by the time we add the extra bedroom. Tony address down by the Humber," I said, subduing a belch, mentioned the place had a stone fountain.

"What's with you and fountains, anyway?" Dennis pointed his Rolling Rock at the one on the hutch.

I said it was a Zen thing.

"Well, it's nice you found a little place," Debra said. "It's good to dream." Then she was telling Ann about this decorator, guy called Vicente, saying, "Got him busy redoing our place. Turquoise with mauve tones, a southwestern motif. New oak trim. So lucky he could squeeze me in, the man's so in demand." Saying there was talk of a feature in *House Beautiful*.

Belching Rolling Rock and cabbage, I bet there were no Yupik dolls on the woman's mantel. Featured in *House Beautiful*, big fucking deal, and I might have said something if the toilet hadn't flushed from down the hall, followed by a loud thump, followed by Dennis Jr. wailing for help.

The first to jump up, I dashed out, followed by Dennis, the two of us rushing down the hall, hearing overflowing water, a lot of water.

Unlocking the passenger door, I reached in the glovebox, taking out the cigar box and offering one to Dennis, saying, "Hope the swelling goes down."

"Ah yeah, the kid's a good healer," he said, taking one, adding, "Think he'd know not to flush something like that down a toilet." Holding the cigar up to the coach light, moths flitting around, he said, "Good stogie, huh?"

"The kind Churchill smoked." Snipping and priming mine, reaching in and pressing in the car lighter, waiting and lighting us up.

"Times I wonder what goes through the kid's mind." Sticking the cigar in his mouth, Dennis puffed, saying, "Cubans still illegal?"

"In the States maybe, not here," I said. "Top of that, we're burning the evidence, right?"

He puffed and grinned, taking in the Gran Fury, saying again, "Good to see things're looking up for you."

"Waded through enough shit in my time, as you know. I bet you heard most of it, the family pipeline, huh?" I puffed, knowing Debra never missed a chance to take a jab at me, saying I heard he was selling his outfit, trying to swing the conversation back around to investing in the AutoPark.

"Some chemical bigwig's been in touch, wants a couple of my patents," he said. "Talking an all-or-nothing type of deal. Got my lawyer looking it over. Feel like I'm bogged in legalese."

The clamor of header pipes and a bass thump had me turning. Rolling up in his borscht-colored Firebird, Dmitri Kovach parked on my boulevard, fat slicks on the new-mowed grass. Shutting her off, he got out and flicked a wave, maybe with the middle finger up, I couldn't tell.

I said to Dennis, "So you sell it off, then what, guess you two'll be swinging on the golf course, huh?"

"More like taking swings at each other."

"Come on, Deb's so easygoing." I was going for sincere, watching Tibor's kid walk next door, saying, "Ask me, you two'll be living the life. Laughing all the way to the bank."

"That woman laughs, it's on account of whatever she's on."

"Meds, Deb? You kidding?"

"Elavil for her, Ritalin for the kid." He blew a smoke ring at a moth getting too close, saying, "Fuck knows what Mother Hibbit's on."

"Never have guessed," I said. "Well, Mother Hibbit, maybe."

Both of us grinning, puffing the Cubans, each with a can of Rolling Rock. Could hear Debra cackle at something from inside the living room.

Telling me he'd think over the car deal, Dennis said, "Oh, and a word to the wise . . ."

"Yeah?"

"Biggest regret of my life was adding the damned room in the basement of the old place. Mother coming to help out back when Deb was due. Settled in and still no sign of her ever leaving. Moved when we moved. The new place is even bigger." Running a hand through his receding hair, he said, "I were you, leave it cold and fucking dank, my man. Make a friend of mold. Know what I'm saying?"

"Jeez, yeah." I hadn't thought of that, but it sent a chill. Told him I owed him one.

"Last thing you need's another sentence, am I right? Last one was eighteen months, and they let you out. This one . . ." He shook his head.

"Getting off lucky."

"You said it."

The front door opened, and Ann called from the porch, saying she had Penny on the line, wanting me to take it.

Leaving him standing by the car, I laid the cigar on the fender and went down the hall to the office, closing the door, picking up the phone on the combo fax machine, saying, "Hey, Penny, what's up?"

"Seller's agent called. They got another offer coming in," Penny saying it was cash and clean, with no clauses, adding, "Time to make your move, Jeff. Put it on paper."

"Shit." I thought a moment, saying, "You got to buy me some time. Haven't got to the bank yet."

"Not going to work, Jeff."

"Family reunion's taking all my time. Woman's got me running around like a caterer." Ann sending me after cheese, Cornish hens and other groceries. Stopping for a case of beer and a box of wine.

"Got to be on paper, Jeff. The way it works."

"Okay, how about you come over first thing Monday."

"For real, Jeff."

"Just draw it up, and I'll sign it." I needed to call the bank first thing Monday, scrape together the cash I had stashed. Get Ted to write me a puffed-up letter of projected earnings.

"Do what I can, but be better if we go in over asking, show some good faith," she said.

"How's that negotiating?"

"With multiple offers, Jeff, it's how we play it."

"So, okay, make it conditional on financing or something."

"At this point, best if we go in clean, but, it's up to you. I'm just advising here."

"Okay, fine, go an extra . . . uh . . . twenty-five hundred."

"Uh uhn."

"Make it five then."

"Ten'd be better, Jeff."

"Better for who?"

"We could keep looking, sure something'll turn —"

"Fine, go ten."

She said it would be best if she wrote it up and swung by in an hour.

"Can't, told you we got damn company. Got to be Monday."

"Hate to see you lose it, time being of the essence . . ."

"Just work some magic, Penny. It's what you do, right?"

"More like asking for a miracle, but okay, look, I'll make the call, see what I can do. Meantime, you know any prayers . . ."

Setting the receiver down, I grabbed a couple more cold ones and went out through the garage, avoiding the questioning look from Ann, taking my cigar off the hood, having to relight it.

"Something wrong?" Dennis said, taking the beer can.

"Naw, all good." I watched a pair of oncoming headlights climbing the hill, thinking with my luck it was the two mutts in the grey van. Opening the door again, I reached for the Ruger under the ownership papers in the glovebox.

A pickup drove past, the neighbor from up the block, Mike's Yardworks written down the side, a couple of Lawn-Boys sticking out the back.

I guess Dennis saw the pistol, saying, "Got a neighbor from hell?"

"Naw, we just take Block Watch serious around here." I slapped the glovebox shut and popped the tab on my can, saying, "Cheers, man."

. . . BENT BOYS

The Love Boat's neon sign flashed *all girls, all day, all night.*
All day in red, *all night* in blue. Best T&A to go with your
roast-beef buffet. All you can eat — five bucks. Tuck a few
more bucks in a G-string and you got a girl in your lap,
wiping the gravy from your chin.

Jerrel Bent didn't care about any of that. He walked
around the place, into the alley out back. He slipped on the
gloves, allowing Errol "Blue Eyes" and James "Dirty Leg"
time to go in the front door, show themselves by the buffet.
Two of the Dreads were known to frequent a ringside table,
the two likely responsible for putting the hit on his brother.
Jerrel betting they'd make for the exit sign when they saw
his boys step to the buffet. "Heartache Tonight" was throbbing through the PA inside.

Getting a nose full of urine and excrement, Jerrel held
his pistol down along his side, waiting in the dark. The
back-door light cast long shadows. Jerrel stood opposite, by
the graffiti-covered wall, looking at the storm door with its
torn screen hanging loose. The door itself looked reinforced,

likely fitted with a couple of extra deadbolts. Just that kind of neighborhood.

Jerrel got set. This was for Dustin, his older brother, gunned down out front of the Westdale Regent, a five-star in downtown Steeltown. Word was, the doorman had been tipped, standing there and holding the door and putting on a smile. Dustin taking the steps with a blonde on his arm. Waiting for the valet to bring his Lincoln Town Car around front. Jerrel's guys finding out it was a hot jacked-up Toronado that pulled up out front, the tinted window rolling down, two guys inside, one with his hands on the wheel, the passenger shoving a .45 out the window. Dustin going down with three slugs in the chest, the girl and the valet killed, too. Jerrel sent Blue Eyes and Dirty Leg to take care of the doorman before his brother was even in the ground. Put a bounty on the shooters in the Toronado.

Hearing the bolt thrown back, Jerrel raised the barrel, and the two men stepped in front of him, one looking inside over his shoulder.

The first shot killed Emmett Grange, one of the higher-ups of the Dreads, the man who likely gave the order. The second man spun and got his hand in his jacket. Then froze, staring at Jerrel behind the gun barrel.

"You know me?" Jerrel said.

The guy bobbed his head, looking scared, hand still in the jacket, saying he had nothing to do with what went down at the Regent. He jerked a pistol from inside the jacket, and Jerrel shot him. Felt good doing it. Dirty Leg coming out and closing the door behind him, stepping over the bodies, not bothering to look down. Blue Eyes had gone to get the car.

Jerrel tossed the pistol on the bodies, and the two of them walked from the alley.

. . . HARD AND FAST

Walking into Ted's office, I looked at him and sat next to Vick.

Vick said to him, "So, what's up?"

"Got the dark roast." Ted pointed to the takeout tray from next door.

Grabbing one, Vick twisted his neck and checked out the *Sun* on the desk, the headline about a loan shark gunned down in his living room, naming Malcolm Rocca and a known associate, also killed.

"Mean your money troubles over, huh?" Vick said, tearing into a packet of Sweet'N Low. The photo of a first responder shrouding the body with a sheet, out in front of Rocca's house.

"Man makes enemies, that line of work," Ted said, nodding at me to take a coffee, saying, "Want the two of you making a run to Poughkeepsie."

"Getting down to it, huh?" Vick said, flipped to page three, looking at the sunshine girl, saying, "Not bad, give her a seven, maybe seven and a half."

Grabbing the paper, Ted tossed it in his trash can, saying, "We be serious here?"

Vick sat.

Sipping coffee, Ted told us about his transport getting hit last week, three dozen guns ripped off, the Bent Brothers pissed off about no delivery.

"So, it was the Bents shot up the place?" Vick said.

"Looks like."

"Jeff gets a car, an office, and I get lead flying by, sitting duck by the window." Shaking his head, Ted said to me, "You believe this guy?"

"So far I just been selling cars," Vick said.

"And not doing too bad at it, making some money, right?" Reaching in a drawer, Ted slid an envelope across the desk, said it was the same as he gave me.

Peeking inside, Vick smiled and said, "Okay, now we're talking." Thumbing the bills, he counted them. Blowing a stream of smoke, he tapped his cigarette over the trash can, saying, "Guess we're getting to it now, huh? The real deal." Making the envelope disappear.

"Nobody hiring cons these days, you boys both forgetting that?" Ted said, clicked the intercom like he forgot Bonnie wasn't there. Then, reaching in his drawer, he took out a gold pen, tapping it on the desk.

"But it's what makes us right for going down there, playing escort on the way back, right?" Vick said.

"This hair crap, want you knocking that shit off," Ted said to him, kept tapping the pen. "Distracting you, embarrassing me."

"That's on the side. Got nothing to say about it." Looking at me, Vick said, "Jump in anytime."

I shrugged, saying to Ted, "These Bent Boys get their guns, then they'll back off, huh?"

"Yeah, that's the deal, back to being happy customers," Ted said, looking from me to Vick. "You two go down, bring the cars back, have things running smooth. Each get another envelope." Ted finished his paper cup and tossed it at the trash. "Anything else you need to know?"

"I'm good," Vick said, dropping his butt in his cup, tossing it in the trash, looking to me, saying, "Strategy meeting's Friday at two. One with Randy's set for Saturday, same time." Winking at Ted, he said thanks for the cash and walked out.

"What meeting?" Ted said, back to tapping the pen.

"Wants me consulting on his hair thing. Got a guy he wants me to meet, guy might invest," I said, smiling. "A chance to make use of those prison reform courses I took."

Ted not smiling, face turning red.

"Probably not gonna go," I said.

"Yeah, you are. Want you to keep an eye on him."

"The guy's just spinning, like you said."

"Look . . ." Ted dropped his elbows on his desk, saying, "Somebody knew the when and where and hit the carrier. Knew right where to find the guns . . ."

"What, think it was Vick ratted?"

He snapped the pen in half, looked at it starting to drip ink on his fingers and tossed it at the trash.

We sat quiet, Ted pulling a bottle from his bottom drawer, reached a couple glasses next to the Sony, poured and slid one to me, downed his in a gulp, refilled his glass. Finishing my coffee, finally I said, "Was thinking of a guy for this, a legit investor. But maybe with the turn of events . . ." I glanced at the *Sun* in the trash, the headline about Mal Rocca getting killed, saying, "Guessing you don't need it no more."

He looked at me. "Cash investor?"

"Kind of like a brother-in-law, thought I might be able to swing him."

Taking a tissue from the drawer, Ted rubbed the ink from his fingers, saying, "This brother-in-law, he got the kind of dough we'd be talking?"

"Why else we be talking?" Giving him some attitude, I downed my drink, decided now wasn't the time to bring up a finder's fee.

After a moment, he smiled, poured another round, reaching a couple of Cohibas from a box in his top drawer and handed me one, getting his cutter and silver lighter, his initials on the lid.

The two of us lighting up.

Ted saying, "Prison reform courses, huh?"

. . . TO THE MAXX

Tobacco haze hung like a canopy, Vick was drinking from an oversized mug, *Maxx* printed on its glazed side. Sitting across from him, Jackie Delano sported a sweater with a line of Westies crossing her gut. Her mouth working on Doublemint, not up and down, but on a diagonal. Kind of like this alpaca I saw once on *Wild Kingdom*. Perched on a metal stool, me in my new suit I'd just picked up from Walter the tailor, I said to Vick, "No cardboard desk and chair, huh?"

"Desks went up in the fire, and the chairs all got sold out at this outdoor Molson festival. Remember the Five Man Electrical Band, long-haired freaky-people number? Anyway, did this revival tour, put on hell of a show. Printed their song lyrics on the chairs and got them laminated, went like shit through a goose."

Sticking a cigarette in her mouth, Jackie flicked Vick's desk lighter — a big lucite cube done to look like a big casino die — the flame whooshing up, the woman snapping her head back. "Jesus fucking . . ." Dropping the lighter, tossing the charred smoke in the ashtray. "The fuck's with you and fire?"

"Sorry, meant to . . ." Taking it, Vick tapped the lighter on his desk, testing the wheel with his thumb, adjusting it and flicking the flame, handing it back. "There. Flint thing gets stuck sometimes."

Pulling a fresh one from the pack, she stuck it in her mouth. Me, I fanned the air, thinking my suit would smell like shit.

"Not gonna start up, are you?" she said, pushing a smile, saying, "Ted let you drive one off the lot, huh?" Followed by a kissy sound.

Grinning, Vick said to her, "Randy tell you I scored his Jag?"

"That old shitbox?"

"Okay, needs a bit of work, but she's a classic, you ask me."

"Thing needs sand tossed on it, is what." She spoke with the unlit smoke bobbing between her lips, shaking her head, looking over my suit, sour look on her face.

"Anyway, he's towing her over Monday," Vick said.

Reaching in her satchel, she fumbled a stack of pages, tapped them on the desk, spilling half on the floor. "Ah, shit."

Vick bent and scooped pages off the floor. Pulling up the knees of my trousers, I reached for a couple under the desk. The snap of teeth had me jerking back, yelping. Vick's schnauzer snarled and leaped for a better hold. Had me up and dancing the two-step, flicking a leg, the dog snapping its jaws, getting mostly air.

Coming around the desk, Vick caught the dog by the collar, him laughing, saying, "Whoa there, girlie. Let go of Jeff. Come on now."

Head-shaking like she was saying no, the dog kept her jaws locked on my fine Egyptian-cotton cuff, snarling and spitting.

Coaxing the dog to let go, Vick made baby talk, "That's a good girl."

"Good, what the hell's good?" I was checking my pants, punctured and slobbered. "Fuckin' tailor-made." Drawing a tissue from the box on the desk, I wiped at it, hoping Walter could do something about the holes.

"Not into dogs, huh, Jeff?" Jackie said, enjoying this.

"Not ones that bite me, no."

"Ought to know better than stick your hand in a strange dog's face."

"Didn't know he even had one."

She went about straightening and sorting, spreading pages on the desk, slipping on her glasses, asking me, "Need a Band-Aid or something 'fore I go on?"

"Tetanus shot might be nice." Sitting back on the stool, I blotted at my pant leg.

"Anyway, was about to say our potential's bigger than I realized." Still grinning as she read from a page, "Sixty million hair-loss sufferers and three hundred thousand salons. Means we're gonna sell a shitload at the Hairdressers' Show."

"That's your stat, a shitload?" I said.

"What I call plain English."

"Hey, come on, guys," Vick said, getting the dog to settle back under his desk, trying to lighten things, asking her, "Any response from the Jays?"

"Still waiting."

"The Blue Jays?" I asked.

"Got a problem with them, too?" Jackie said, the cigarette bobbing.

"Just, pro athletes get big bucks."

"Except when me and the GM's old lady are like this." Holding up two nicotine-stained fingers. "Been doing her half-updo since . . . like forever."

"Gonna offer them shares," Vick said, "same as our Elvis."

"Giving Archie shares?" I said.

Ignoring me, Jackie saying to Vick, "Oh, I might have us hooked up with an outfit doing high-tech follicle testing. See if they're willing to go fifty/fifty on the booth." Sticking a fresh cigarette in her mouth, she turned to me, saying, "You know, Jeff, getting kind of tired of your high-and-mighty and tailor-made. You don't want to do this, nobody's holding a gun to your head . . . yet."

I started to say I was here paying Vick a courtesy, Tina picking the moment for a second lunge. Leaning forward for the desk lighter, Vick flicked it for Jackie, trying to block Tina with his shoe. He shifted the lighter, and the flame singed Jackie's hair as she leaned in and puffed.

Jumping back, she lost the cigarette, throwing wild slaps at her head, smelling her hair on fire, yelling, "Hair . . . fuck . . . fire!"

Flicking a foot at the dog, I grabbed a handful of her pages and swatted at Jackie's head, knocking the cigarette away. Fast thinking.

Not thinking, Vick tossed his coffee, coming around and catching hold of Tina.

Hair matted to her head, Jackie slung herself back in the chair and sputtered coffee. Not saying a word, she sat dripping, eyes burning holes, and began cleaning her glasses on the Westies sweater, her hair looking like doused brushfire.

Checking for tooth marks on my fine cotton, I glanced at her, the woman tossing her coffee-soaked pages in the trash bin, getting up without a word and clomping up the stairs.

"That woman's got issues," I said.

"That may be," he said, straightening the lighter on the desk, "but trust me, Maxx is gonna take off. Issues or not."

. . . THE BLUE PLATE

Fastening his belt, Ted smiled at the girl the escort service had sent to the condo at Harbour Square. Didn't matter her real name wasn't Ginger. Tall, young and with a waist he could almost get his hands around. The two of them had talked over drinks first, Ginger smiling perfect teeth at him. Bright and charming. Made him forget he was just a john. Forgetting about his troubles with Liz, his wife.

Checking his watch, he offered Ginger a lift, taking her down to parking, getting in his car. An hour before meeting Liz for dinner, the two of them hoping to divide their property without the need of blood-sucking lawyers. Maybe they'd reminisce about Jenny when she was a kid, back when times were better. That kind of talk always softened Liz, brought her back to better times, times before she got her edge. Maybe she'd spend the night at the condo. It had happened twice before. Then she'd be gone again, driving back to the country place they'd bought out by the Bay of Quinte. Spend her time digging in her garden.

En route up Bay, he turned at Nathan Phillips Square and dropped Ginger out front of the Sheraton, guessed she had another john, watched till he lost sight of her inside the doors. He was heading over to University when he spotted the grey van a couple cars back, two guys inside, guessing it was the ones Jeff told him about. Tailing him now.

The traffic was light this time of night. Ted drove in the opposite direction from his place. Reaching in the glovebox, he got on Front and drove west. Turned at Bathurst and took the Lakeshore where the Gardiner loomed above him. Thinking how to play it, he slowed as he rolled by the CNE. Pressing down his window, he let the van pull alongside. The guy on the passenger side cranked down his window, smiling down at Ted, saying, "Know who we are, right?"

Holding the wheel with his left hand, Ted put his right hand across his forearm, steadied the Ruger and fired a round through their side door. Didn't say a word, just watched the van swerve then screech off. These two morons slow getting the word that Mal Rocca's ticket had been punched, the two of them out of work. Ted guessed that ought to take care of it.

. . . MEAT WAS HERE

"Guy goes by Meat Loaf," Vick said, handing me a beer in a glass, "you know, the *Bat Out of Hell* guy."

I just looked at him. The man wearing a camel blazer with the patches on the elbows over a white turtleneck, Levi jeans and Roots shoes, the kind that looked like the heels were in the front.

"Ought to turn on a radio sometime," he said, the two of us clinking glasses. "Anyway, Ricki heard it from a waiter." His date was into the guy's music, hoping to get an autograph.

I thanked Vick for the beer he'd brought from the open bar, watched him go back over to Ricki on the other side of the long table. She was a dirty blonde packed into a tight black number, her heels putting her eye-level with Vick. Hand on his arm, she giggled at something he was saying. I guessed her to be a hooker, at least an indebted affair. Couldn't see something like that going for a broke middle-aged ex-con losing his surfer hair.

A squad of servers in white jackets juggled trays of hors d'oeuvres and champagne in flutes, rushing in and out. The private room at Valencia's was hopping with a mix of Ted's family and friends. Stepping next to Ann, I made some small talk with Bonnie and her fiancé, Allen, some runt of an ex-jockey. I asked Bonnie about coming back to work. "You kidding?" Bonnie talking about the showroom getting shot up.

Guessing I'd have to explain why I hadn't mentioned it to Ann later, I asked Allen about his horse racing days, the guy talking a blue streak about that post-time feeling, how many mounts he'd raced at Woodbine and Fort Erie, coming in second behind Sandy Hawley, missing that win by a nose.

Trying not to yawn, I finished my beer. Ann tugged me away, the two of us stepping to the bar for refills. Ann asking why I didn't tell her about the showroom getting shot up.

"The way you worry?"

Rolling her eyes, she said we'd talk more later.

Waiters corked wine, letting it breathe. Liz Bracey made the rounds, checking the place settings and introducing herself, working the room. Athletic and brunette. A bleached white smile and a firm handshake. The woman looking good for near fifty.

Ted had confided over corned beef and pickles at *Deli*-cious that the two of them were in a marital sandtrap, pretty much giving up on trying to revive the spark, not seeing much of each other these days. Liz had grown weary of taking the back seat to Ted's ventures, mild objection turning to resignation. Moving to the Prince Edward County house, loving that rural elbow-room, Liz dug her hands into the earth while Ted took in his penthouse view of the Toronto Islands. High ceilings and marble counters. Working his deals was in his blood, and lately, I guessed, Ted had been thinking some of it could get spilled, the reason he moved first and stamped out the debt with Mal Rocca.

At the top of the hour, Liz took her spot by the door, signaling for the lights to be turned low, everybody getting set.

A unison of "surprise" as the lights snapped back on, and Ted stood there stutter-stepping like he'd been struck. His daughter, Jenny, steadied him, kept him from bolting for the door. A nice round of applause, then Liz and Jenny led him to the head of the long table.

After a "fuck me" or two under his breath, Ted pulled it together and stuck on that frozen smile of his, holding onto the back of his chair, saying to everybody, "You guys, you're all fired." Saying somebody better get him a drink.

Everyone laughed.

"Should've seen your face," I heard Liz say, brushing her lips against his cheek. "Thought you might keel over."

"No such luck." Ted kissed her back, making it look real.

Liz rubbed a thumb over the lipstick smudge on his cheek, the only color on his face, her other hand patting his chest, looked like she was feeling for a heartbeat through one of Walter's suits.

Leaning close, Ann said, "So, who's the tart?" Flicking her eyes across the table. "One with Vick?"

"Goes by Ricki." I sipped my rum and Coke, saying she was his date. Then accepted a plate of antipasto being passed around, taking a bread stick, and passing the plate to Ann.

"Yeah, but, I mean, who is she? Fake boobs flopping out one end, butt hanging out the other. Not the cockeyed woman you described."

"No, that one's Jackie. One with the hair deal." Biting the

bread stick, I glanced over at Ricki as she stood and tugged at the hem of her dress, pulling away from Vick, starting for the door. Guessing she was going in search of Meat Loaf, get his autograph.

"Well, 'Vick and Rick,' kinda cute, I guess. Still, imagine me walking around dressing like that," Ann said, biting into a chilled prawn, looking for somewhere to put the tail.

The clap on the back had me coughing bread crumbs, my own heart leaping.

"You old dog," Ted said, pumping my hand and squeezing, talking through smiling teeth, "Could've warned me."

"Sworn to secrecy." I smiled, clearing my throat. "But I figured nothing gets by you, right?"

Ted turned to Ann. "Nice to finally put a face to the name, Ann." Still squeezing my hand. "Got to say, you're all this old boy talks about." Finally letting go, he offered Ann his hand.

Switching the prawn tail to her left hand, she let Ted take her hand, saying, "Well, I doubt that, but it's so nice to be included in your special day, Ted."

"You kidding? You people are like family." Letting go of her hand, Ted looked at me. "You're one lucky dog, you know it?"

Ann saying he was too kind.

"Mind if I bend this boy's ear a minute?" Ted said, the frozen smile, taking my sleeve.

"No shoptalk on your birthday." Liz stepped up, the two women smiling and exchanging hellos, taking each other in the way women did.

Ann said, "So, I hear you're quite the gardener, Liz." Something Ted had told me at the deli.

Liz admitted she was, saying it gave her peace. Saying she'd heard we'd been house hunting. Ann telling her about the place with the blue shutters, then saying Jenny was Liz's spitting image. Saying no, we didn't have any of our own yet, but something we were working on.

Ted led me to the far wall, glancing over at Ricki standing by the door, the girl looking up and down the hall. "Was hoping that was gonna jump out of my cake." He watched her walk out the door, then he caught Vick wandering over to his daughter, Jenny sitting alone at the table, Vick introducing himself, asking if she needed a top-up.

"Jesus, so help me . . ." Ted said.

Catching his arm, I stopped him and reached in my pocket, pulling out a slim gift box, trying to fluff the flattened bow, saying, "Liz said not to get you anything, but, well . . ."

"Hey now." Smiling, Ted tore away the wrapping, handed it to me, and opened the box. "Montblanc. Now there's one smart fucking pen." He twisted it a few times, holding it like a dagger, looking over at Vick, saying to me, "Guess I better not snap this one, huh?" Clipping the pen in an inside pocket, handing me the box. Taking out a pair of Cohibas from the same pocket, he said, "Come on, let's go catch some fucking air before we eat."

●

Puffing away, Ted told me what happened on the Lakeshore, how good it felt putting a round through the sheet metal of the grey van. The two of us watching Ricki step past the glass doors, the dress hiking up and her tugging at the hem.

"Suppose they're real?" I asked.

"Either way, world-class tits."

"Meant them being a couple. Girl like that going out with Vick? Maybe pen pals when he was in the joint."

"You kidding? C-note says five bills gets you time on her clock," Ted said. "Something like that lets something like him on top, she's got the meter running, trust me." Ted puffed his cigar to life. "Hooker of the first order. Sure didn't spend his money on clothes, right?"

Vick and Robbie Boyd came out the glass doors, Vick tapping a cigarette from his Player's pack.

"Good of you boys to come," Ted said, offering his hand first to Vick, squeezing it, asking if Robbie was having a change of heart.

"Guess that's you joking, right, Ted?" Robbie shook with his left, taking a smoke from Vick's pack, saying he was surprised he got invited.

"Still think of you as family, Robbie, you know that," Ted said.

Lighting up, Vick said, "Speaking of which, man, that daughter of yours, nice girl and sweet as a peach." Smiling at Ted.

"Don't know about a peach, but let's agree forbidden fruit." Ted looked like he might squash his cigar in the man's mouth.

"And that's one nifty pen, Jeff, a class gift." Vick grinned at me. "Bit ass-kissy you ask me, but, hey . . ."

"Would've got you one, too, Vick," I said, "for your memos, you know. Only trouble, Crayola doesn't make one in your size." First time I realized we were at odds.

"Come on now, boys." Ted laughed, clapping Vick on the back. "How about we cut the crap, at least for tonight?"

"It's your day," Vick said, flicking a match on his thumb-nail for Robbie, smiling, saying, "Hey, you boys seen Ricki around?"

"Hard to miss." Ted pointed through the glass in the direction she had gone. "Nice-looking girl."

"Yeah, she's good people, but kind of obsessed with Meat Loaf being here." Explaining to Ted it was the *Bat Out of Hell* guy. "Gone to get his autograph."

"Gonna ask him to scrawl *Meat was here*," I said, "find a patch of skin somewhere."

Vick gave me a look, like what's with you?

I waved him off, said I was going to the men's. "I see your girl, I'll tell her you're looking." Cupping the stogie in my hand, I held it low on account of the no smoking sign inside the door, asking a busboy to point me to the can.

. . . BRASS RING

Standing before the urinal, feet planted apart, the cigar at the corner of my mouth, the tobacco smoke masking the whiff of the urinal cakes. Subway tiles in front of me looked like they were sweating, the flusher handle, too. No way I was touching that. Not sure why I was ticked off at Vick, I zipped up, thinking I should check the Windsor knot on the new tie, red with blue stripes. Turning, I caught the flash of a ring.

The punch knocked my head into the tiles. The cigar squashed to pulp, sparks jumping before his eyes. I landed in the urinal like it was a seat. Felt the wet. Thinking it was Vick who threw the punch, the crack about Ricki setting him off.

Shaking my head, I pushed up and threw one back, taking another hit to the side of the head. It was Bundy. Felt like he had a roll of quarters in his fist, the floor rushing up, took a kick to the groin.

Bundy and Egg looked down at me as I tried to breathe, tapped my pocket, feeling for the pistol, the one out in the glovebox.

Next thing, I was pulled up by the silk tie and felt myself being shoved toward the service exit, past the guy with the ponytail working the dish pit, the guy barely glancing up from the heat and steam. Bundy saying their buddy was sick on account of the slop they served in this joint. The guy saying yeah, he wasn't surprised.

Pulling back the side door with the bullet hole through it, Bundy shoved me in the grey van, getting in and slamming it behind us. Balls in misery and still dazed, I made a crawl for the back, Egg putting it in gear and driving away from where Ted, Vick and Ronnie stood smoking. Fishing out his pruners, Bundy tossed me down, pinned my shoulders with his knees and was yanking at my belt, saying, "Told you this was to be continued, right? And by fuck, I'm upping the ante."

Sight of the pruners got my adrenaline kicking in. First thing you learned in the Don: you got no choice but to fight, you let out the beast. My fingers went for Bundy's eyes, nails dragging down his face, skin catching under my nails as I bucked him off.

Grabbing the cross from the rearview, Egg growled and swung it, tried gouging me with it but missed.

Landing a big slap to his ear, I felt the van swerve. Egg slammed the brakes and Bundy made another grab. Clutching the hand holding the pruners, I got an elbow up under his nose, feeling the cartilage crunch. Hit Egg on the ear a second time. Losing control, Egg hip-checked a parked car. Thrown around the bare metal interior, I scrambled for the back doors, Egg hitting the gas and Bundy clutching my legs below the knees. I was twisting around as the rear doors flew open, and both of us were pitched out into the street, with me landing on top.

Hosing the sidewalk in front of his fish shop, the store-keeper looked on, two guys spilling into the street, the grey van hopping the curb and taking out a parking meter. A shower of change raining down.

Pushing me off, Bundy got up slow, holding his arm like he'd hurt it, getting to shaky legs and stumbling for the back of the van, climbing in and slamming the door shut. Egg backing off the bent meter, putting her in first and rolling on, a hubcap dropping and wobbling off.

Twisting off the nozzle on the hose, the shopkeeper watched the van drive away, then asked if I was all right.

"Never better, friend," I said, told him we were Hollywood stuntmen, just practicing a scene, nothing to get excited about. Getting to my feet, I groaned, scads of hurt, guessing they might swing around the block and try for round two, these guys not giving up so easy. Nothing felt broken, a torn sleeve, ripped knee, the seat of my pants wet, the suit I just picked up from Walter's. Asking the shopkeeper where I was, I hobbled in the direction of the Valencia, wishing him a good evening, guessing Ann was waiting on me to pick an entrée, then a dessert for sharing.

...NEEDLES AND PINS

The old Norge chugged like it was on its last legs, the vinyl floor vibrating underfoot, Ann saying she was going call the landlord, demand a new dishwasher.

She wasn't buying my story about getting in a fight out back of the restaurant, my cigar smoke bothering the greaser who worked the dish pit. Walking back into the party looking all beat up. Accused me of keeping things from her. Then she was back to looking at the phone, anxious that we hadn't got word from Penny Mansell about our offer.

"Soon as she presents, she'll call," I said, my lip thick and throbbing. I might have got up and paced if it wasn't for the jab in my hip. Think I got that when I flew out of the back of the van. I switched on the kitchen radio, the news anchor talking about another gang shooting out back of a strip club down on King.

Ann telling me to turn it off, saying, "Isn't there enough bad news without that?" She wrung her hands. "Sure we're doing the right thing here, Jeff?" Her eyes scared and pleading.

"It's all you been talking about." Going to the dining room, I picked the makeup mirror off the sill. Out past the brambles, Dmitri's Firebird sat on our boulevard lawn. Damn neighbors. I looked up and down the road.

The ringing phone had me jumping, nearly dropping the mirror, the jab poking through my hip.

●

"Another five? Jesus H . . ." Ann clapped a hand to her chest.

"Not like I had a choice," I said.

Dropping into her chair, she repeated the amount, giving a sharp exhale.

"And it wasn't five, started there, but ended higher."

"How much higher?"

"Ten."

Mouth going into an O, Ann hissed air.

"Was that or we let it go."

Her thumb scraped at the cigarette scab in the Formica.

"It's the sellers, Ann, greedy bastards squeezing every dime."

"But why ten?"

"Penny said it's better."

"Better for who?"

Looking at the clock on the stove, I told her I had to go. Time to head over to Vick's, meet this guy Randy.

"You can't go, not now."

"Gonna all work out. Penny'll get it done. Plus there's nothing more we can do." Grabbing my torn jacket from the hall closet, the Ruger in the pocket, I told her I'd call from Vick's, check in, told her again not to worry.

. . . WITHOUT A NET

"Okay, you squared the debt, I get that," Mateo Cruz said, phoning from the Poughkeepsie shop. Mal Rocca getting his ticket punched. Mateo calling it a step in the right direction, careful what he said on the phone. "Not so sure, sending up more cars right now with no idea who hit the carrier."

"Gonna be worse we do nothing and don't deliver."

"'Less it happens again."

Thinking of what the Bent Boys would do if he didn't deliver, Ted stood, looking from his hundred-and-eighty-degree view. Sun glinting off the water. The sound of the shower spray stopped, and Ginger stepped from the en suite, rubbing herself with the towel, giving him that smile that melted away his years.

"No doubt, we got a leak," Mateo said, "either your end or mine, one we're not plugging."

"Not arguing that, but we got these guys waiting, the kind you don't keep waiting." Ted smiled back at her, taking her in. Man, that smooth skin, those curves. All woman.

"Guess we're fucked either way."

"Sending my guys down," Ted said. "Riding shotgun and taking a new route."

Mateo finally agreeing, not seeing any other way, the Bent Boys wanting the guns they already paid for. Likely hit Bracey harder next time, could send somebody after Mateo, too. "So I'll make the call," Mateo said, meaning Conner, the New York auctioneer, instructing him what to buy. The guy arranging the guns through the Iron Pipeline, too.

"All gonna work out, my man," Ted said, watching Ginger grab her bag, wave to him and walk out the door.

. . . PENNY FOR A POUND

"Leave 'em on," Vick said, looking at my shoes, leading the way down the hall, photos of his ex-wives on the walls, one of them with a girl standing next to her.

Growling aversion, Tina followed a step behind me, sniffing at my ankles. It was a plain bungalow, but Vick had told me in the Don this place was his, all paid for. I sent the dog a mental image: snap at me again and you'll get a taste of shoe leather and a rocket ride across the back fence.

"Vick!" Jackie yelled from beyond the screen door. "Better get out here. She's smoking like a bitch."

Hurrying out the screen, Vick called over his shoulder, "Come on out and meet the guys."

Closing the screen on growling Tina, I stepped onto the deck.

Telling me to grab a brew — smoke pouring from a greasy old Weber, corner of the deck — Vick jerked up the lid, a two-alarm blaze dancing out. Jumping back, he snatched long tongs, darting in and out of the licking flames, trying to rescue a half dozen patties, plunking them on a platter, saying over his shoulder, "Everybody like 'em well done?"

"Told you to go with the lean," Jackie said, sitting at the picnic table. "Gonna burn your place to the fucking ground, buying that cheap crap."

Three men sat around a folding table, grinning and looking more like thugs than investors, all big, all in tight tees, tats over biceps. All looking at me. Empty bottles of Molson's circling a sample box of Maxx.

"Randy, Pony, Luther," Jackie pointed around the table, then at me. "Jeff." Looking at me like she had shit in her mouth, she swigged her beer, hair looking as if somebody took a scythe to it and hacked off the singed spots. Jackie in a widow-maker, her jug tits sagging and misshaping the graphic of Ozzy Osbourne, a nipple stabbing at the first O in Ozzy.

Randy rose to his feet, a tower of about two hundred and fifty pounds. Sticking out a hand, wrist tattooed with a skull surrounded by barbed wire and flames, Jackie's name in green on the back of the hand.

I shook the hand.

"On account of you her hair caught fire," he said.

"Me?" I looked at her, then Vick, saying, "More about Vick's lighter going off like his barbecue."

"But you got her distracted," Randy said, then clapped my arm, saying, "Just funning with you, brother."

Pony and Luther were grinning, looking at her hair.

Coming with the platter of charred burgers, Vick set it next to a basket of buns, flies walking between sesame seeds. He swished a hand overtop, the flies disturbed and landing on the sliced tomatoes and onion.

Picking up a patty, Randy looked at it and tossed it back, picked up another and stuck it in a bun, offering it to me. "Here you go, bro. Burnt shit bothers you, just scrape it off."

Should have just taken it, but I told him I didn't eat red meat.

"Don't eat meat?" He looked surprised.

"Some, but not red."

"Nothing red about it," Pony said, frowning at his own patty crusted in black, sticking it between a bun and going for the condiments.

Luther asked, "What the fuck you eat, then?" Randy saying something about surviving in a place like the Don on just beans and veggies.

Telling them I went with chicken, sometimes fish, I dragged a metal deck chair close to the picnic table, slung my jacket over it, saying something about beans had all kinds of protein. The jacket felt light, and I felt uneasy, the Ruger out under the seat of the Gran Fury. Didn't think I'd need it at an investors' meeting, before seeing these guys.

Pointing to the garnish, Vick said, "Toss yourself a salad, you want." Enjoying my discomfort.

Luther and Pony grinning some more.

"And grab a brew — you drink it, right?" Randy said, pointing over to the Igloo cooler.

"Yeah, could use a beer." Going to it, I fished out a dripping Export.

Jackie doused her burger, plastic squeeze bottle farting, and smiled at me.

Popping the tab, I took a sip, froth going over the side.

Wondering about these guys, Vick going back and lining a second round of patties on the grill, the flames under control now.

Luther was talking about the chili burgers at this joint called the Apache, saying they were the best in town. Saying he had a good mind to go over and pick up a takeout bag full.

"That old fuck at the Apache sweats like a pig over his grill, man," Jackie said, taking a bite, going on, "Watched the guy, got beads of sweat coming off that hook nose, rolling down and dripping on the meat. How's the guy not notice something like that?"

"Still beats this burned shit." Luther swallowed a bite and shot Vick a look.

"So, you in the Don, uh, same time as Vick?" Randy said. "Marcel putting you boys in the used-car biz."

"Yeah, something like that," I said, looking at Vick, wondering how much he told these guys, adding, "We got some history." Drinking some beer, I asked Randy what line he was in.

"Well, towing pays the bills." Throwing a thumb at Pony, saying they were partners. "And Luther — well, mostly we just ride."

"Guessing you go with the hard sell, huh?" Pony said, tapping his own lip, looking at my bruised cheek and fat lip.

"Yeah, do whatever it takes," I said.

Taking a patty, Randy stuck it on a bun and blasted mustard at it, the glop squishing from the sides of the bun, then bit into it.

"Nice ride out front. That yours?" I asked him, sipping, trying to get the attention off me.

"Yup, vintage FXR." Randy holding the burger away so the dripping fat and bits of condiments landed on the deck.

"Low-end torque that baby pumps out," Jackie said, clapping a hand on Randy's thigh. "Harley's the second best thing a man can put between his legs, that right, babe?" Randy mumbling, "You bet" around a bite, Jackie sending me a mayo air-kiss.

Shoving himself up, Luther told her to play nice, saying he had to piss. Cramming the last of his burger in his mouth.

"How about use the john this time." Jackie nodded to the screen door. "I'm eating here."

Opening the screen door, Luther said something about her acting like the queen of England and stepped inside. Tina scrambled out past him, zeroing in on me, growling and showing teeth, dancing a circle around my ankles.

"No, you don't." Scooping her up and saving me from doing a jig in front of these guys, Vick clapped a hand over her muzzle, saying, "No biting Jeff. Come on now, girlie."

"Hey, killer." Randy patted the dog, tearing off a piece of patty and feeding it to her. To me, he said, "Not a dog guy, huh?"

I just sucked some beer.

Tucking her back inside, Vick told her to behave. Tina whimpering and scratching at the screen.

Picking up the bottle of Maxx, Randy looked at it, then at me, saying, "Want to hear it from you, Jeff, how this shit's supposed to grow hair."

"My thing's the cars. I'm just here consulting. Want the short strokes, you got to talk to Vick or . . ." Glancing at Jackie.

The woman smiling, enjoying the unease I couldn't hide.

Looking at the bottle of Maxx, Randy said he wasn't all the way convinced.

"The shit works," she told him, taking the bottle from him, saying the test results were off the charts, adding, "Why I want you in the game, honey."

"You got test results?" Randy said.

"I say it if we didn't?" Jackie with her hand on his thigh.

"I put money in this," Randy said, "it won't be no game. Besides, you got no contract with the inventor guy?"

"Made a verbal agreement, guy giving me his word, same thing," she said.

"Verbal, that's worth shit." Downing his beer, he looked around from me to Vick, told Vick to fetch him another one.

"'Cept I give pretty good verbal, right?" she said to Randy, the woman working her tongue between her molars, sucking at bits of meat, patting his big leg.

Reaching in the cooler, Vick handed Randy a dripping Ex, saying, "We hit the trade show, man, Maxx'll be flying off the shelves, sure of that."

"And if it don't?"

"Then you get your money back," Vick said, looking from him to me, then to her.

"That goes without saying, amigo," Randy said.

Coming out the screen door, Luther zipped up his fly, fishing the last cold one from the Igloo, flicking water from his hand, reaching and sticking the last patty between the last bun. Telling Vick he was out of beer.

"Take some Maxx home, give it a try, any of you guys,"

Vick said, catching Tina, setting her on his lap, telling her to settle down, the dog growling my way.

"We look like we need more hair?" Pony said.

Randy looked at Jackie, the woman doing her oral hygiene, then back at me, saying, "So, these cars, you buy 'em at auction, huh, get them detailed, put them on a trailer, send them north and bank on a good exchange?"

"Yeah, basically how it works," I said.

"Way I hear it, you and Vick're going down this week," he said, "see things running smooth. Coming back with a full load."

"Heard that, huh?" I glanced at Vick, got the feeling this wasn't about these guys investing in the hair product, caught a look passing between Luther and Pony. Vick looking jumpy, asking if anybody wanted more meat.

. . . ANY NAKED EYE

The garage door hung open, the old Jag was an xj, circa the last ice age, mostly racing green but partly rust, with cardboard under its crankcase, oil dripping like lifeblood. Vick's Dodge sat in the driveway behind it.

Pony and Luther pulled away in the tow truck, Randy roaring away on the Harley, Jackie on the back, hanging on. Tina scratching and whining at the door leading from the house.

"So, what's with giving that guy a personal guarantee?" I said, taking my jacket off, slinging it over a shoulder. "Can't back shit like that up."

"What's it to you?"

I shrugged, the two of us looking at the junkyard Jag, its ragtop patched with fabric tape, rear quarter panel suffering terminal rust, tires worn past the treads.

Then I said, "It was you, huh?"

"Me what?"

"This what you got, selling Ted out?" I flicked a finger at the tape, laid the jacket on the hood. "Gave up the time and place, cars coming across the border, and the guy throws in a car, such as it is."

It took a moment, then he said, "Wasn't like that." He hesitated, tapping the toe of his shoe against the rear tire, then said, "Five grand just for the time and place, that or they'd take a drill to my knee. Got any idea about that?"

"Ask Ted's driver Bucky, one that got laid up. Word is he's going to be walking funny and with a stick from here on. Ask me, that's on you."

"Look, you want, I'll split it with you?"

"And half the guilt comes with it."

"Ted's just in it for Ted, you got to know that, right, even with your head up the man's ass?"

Didn't think about it, I just threw the fist, the right sending Vick to the concrete. I stood, shaking the pain from my knuckles.

Holding the side of his face, he looked up. "It's like that, huh? Got the Chuvalo over your desk, makes you kinda punchy." Pushing himself up, he threw one back, the two of us trading punches, grunting and grappling over the oil stain, Vick twisting me around and putting on a headlock. Me clutching at his arm, the other hand catching a tangle of surfer hair.

The vw pulling up the driveway got him letting go. Both of us standing, brushing at our clothes, Vick smoothing his hair. Skinny tires crunching on the gravel. Vick straightened his shirt, putting on a welcome smile. Licking blood from my lip, I ran a hand through my own hair.

Switching off the engine, Ricki flipped the visor down

and checked herself in the vanity before putting a heel out on the gravel, skimpy shorts this time, saying, "Interrupting something, boys?"

"Guys just being guys, you know." Vick walked over, hugging her, Ricki turning a cheek for him to kiss.

Saying, "Hi Jeff," she pointed to my ripped shirt, a couple of buttons missing, then saying to Vick, "You're not going looking like that." His collar hung like a flap. "Gonna catch a powder, give you time to change." Careful where she stepped, she threw a dark look my way, her heels tapping the concrete. She opened the kitchen door, and Tina charged out, growling, Vick catching her in a midair leap, saying, "No, baby, think Jeff's had all he can handle."

Licking my lip, I snagged my jacket, tried not to limp, thinking if it wasn't for the beating I had already taken at Valencia's, I would have shown him something, saying, "Lucky she came by when she did. Best money you spent all day."

"Meaning what?"

I shrugged. "And your car's a piece of shit." Rapping my knuckles on the fender.

"Just needs a tune-up, like I just gave you."

"Ask me, thing needs recycling." Cursing the limp, I went down the driveway, reaching for my keys.

"You change your mind," he called, "still work something out."

Opening the Gran Fury's door, I checked up the road. Feeling a stab in my side as I got in and stuck in the ignition key and turned it on.

... LIKE IN MINSK

A guy was dropping off an envelope, Ted wanting me to hang on to it. That's all he said, left me a message on my machine, gave me a number for a car phone in case the guy didn't show by noon. Didn't leave a name. Writing the number down, I figured it had to be money for guns.

My own check plus the twenty-five hundred sat on the Formica table, making the downstroke for the house, Penny Mansell coming by to pick it up, should have been here an hour ago. I looked at the clock, needing to get to the bank, see the assistant manager and sign the papers before they closed.

Running my tongue along the split lip, I thought about the house. Never owned a place of my own, never got that feeling of pride people talked about. Just the dread of property taxes and mortgage payments. The thought of either had me feeling like I was wearing that clip-on tie again, being choked. No joy in following a Lawn-Boy on Saturday mornings, rows made by the wheels going back and forth, smelling my own cut grass. Climbing a ladder and pulling handfuls of decaying leaves from the gutters, draining algae from the fountain, mortaring the pecker back on the cherub.

Always fixing something. Owning a piece of the rock was resting heavy on my chest.

Ann was over there now, head librarian Pritchard giving her the morning off, the sellers allowing Ann in to take measurements. Ann deciding between mini-blinds or drapes, paint or wallpaper. The woman in seventh heaven.

The knock at the door felt like a jolt. Stepping to the front hall, I checked the peephole.

Penny Mansell stood with a folder under her arm. Swinging back the door, I smiled and took the deposit check and cash and handed it to her.

Looking it over, she tapped a finger at it, looking sour, saying, "Supposed to be certified, Jeff. Sure I said that."

"Yeah, just ran short of time. Figure the cash makes up for it, shows goodwill, all that. Look, Penny, I'm good for it, trust me." Then I turned it around, saying I wanted to add a clause, wanting the sellers fixing the fountain.

"The what?"

"Cherub, thing on the fountain, part of it's busted off. Want it fixed."

"I go back with that, you wanting to add a clause, on top of no certified funds? My broker'll have me for lunch."

"Had damned company, remember? Bad timing all the way around. Look, just put it in, okay? Think I know what I'm doing."

"Fine. May I?" Forcing a smile, she stepped past me and took the wall phone and punched in a number, unable to reach the selling broker, hanging up and telling me, "Do what I can to stall, Jeff, but meantime, roll the cash into it, the whole thing needs to be certified." Asking the girl on the other end of the line to put her through to Bette, the office administrator, telling me while she waited I had to get the certified funds today, handing the check and cash back. She told Bette on the other end to add the clause, dictating it over the phone, told her thanks, then she hung up. Giving me another one of her cards, she walked out toward her ragtop Benz, a black Suburban rolling across the bottom of the driveway, blocking her in, a guy in the passenger seat looking up, checking the house numbers. Two black guys dropping off Ted's envelope. The guys I'd been hearing about on the news, Bent Boys shooting up the whole town. Maybe Ted's way of letting me edge closer to the real business.

Stepping to the closet, I tucked the Ruger in the belt behind my back and went to the welcome mat. The passenger stepped out, a leather jacket, twin earrings and shades, walking up the drive, nodding to Penny as she passed, the driver rolling the Suburban back, letting her back out. Don't know why, but I jotted their plate number on the back of Penny's card, tucked it away.

"You Bracey's man, uh?" Errol "Blue Eyes" Ealy coming to the stoop, an easy way about him. He reached inside his jacket, my own hand going around my back.

"Easy, my man. Just bringing you some lettuce. Sure your man Bracey gave you word, uh?" He handed me a thick envelope. James "Dirty Leg" Freeze pulled to the bottom of the driveway, got out and came up, looking at me, saying to his buddy, "This white boy look like he gonna jump."

"Hey!" Tibor Kovach tossed down his rake and shoved his way through the hedge, cutting across the lawn. Both men turning and reaching inside their jackets.

"Not a good time, Tibor," I said, flapping the envelope against my open palm.

Tibor saying he wanted these boys to cut it nice and short, pointing to the cedars out front.

They looked at each other, Dirty Leg saying to him, "Boys? We look like the hired help, uh? Two brothers dressed sharp and stepping from a ride worth more than your house. And you guessing us yardies got the Lawn-Boy in back of the truck, uh?"

"Just say when you do it?" Tibor said, not hearing him, pointing at the unruly hedge.

"You keep talking, it's gonna be coming right up," Dirty Leg said.

"Got to be done," Tibor said, slapping the back of one hand into the palm of the other.

"Maybe we let you gents work it out," Blue Eyes said, nodding at Dirty Leg, turning to go, saying to me, "We be in touch. Give you an estimate."

"No." Tibor pointed at me, saying, "He pays." Stuck out a big palm, pressing it against Dirty Leg's chest, blocked him from leaving.

Backing a step, looking at him, Dirty Leg said, "I got to ask you to step aside, maybe we not gonna be friends."

Brow crinkling, Tibor took hold of Dirty Leg's hand, turning it palm up, saying, "Not hands of man who works. Woman's hands."

"You believe this shit?" Dirty Leg said to Blue Eyes, yanking his hand back, pointing a finger, saying to Tibor, "Best you go rake up your leaves, before you be lying under them."

Sure wasn't expecting Tibor to take a swing — the way they handled things in Minsk — catching Dirty Leg solid, knocking him flat. Blue Eyes jumping at me, keeping me from getting my pistol. Going for his own.

Dirty Leg was slow pushing himself up, throwing his own fist. Shuffling back, then in again, Tibor used his size and countered with a roundhouse, knocking Dirty Leg back down.

Jamming my Ruger under Blue Eyes' chin, I said, "So we're clear, man's got nothing to do with me." I felt his own barrel in my gut. Him saying to me, "Still, we dancing now, uh, white bread?"

I eased up, pointed the gun away, then he did, too, both of us looking to the street, putting our pistols away. The hedge blocking most of the scene from the neighbors.

Tibor yanked Dirty Leg up, saying to him, "Now, you boys take care of hedge, and give good price."

Blue Eyes stepping in, keeping Dirty Leg from pulling his pistol.

I said to Blue Eyes, "Ought to try living next door to him."

"You want, I can plug him one," Dirty Leg said, shaking Blue Eyes off.

"Wouldn't do any good," I said.

"Man's in need of some kind of help." Blue Eyes shrugged, hooked Dirty Leg by the sleeve, turning his man back toward the Suburban, Dirty Leg calling over his shoulder to Tibor, "Next time, we do it for real."

Waving him off, Tibor gave me a sour look, then turned and crossed the lawn, muttering in Belarusian.

Waiting till they drove off, I looked at the sealed envelope in my hand, then over at Tibor getting back to raking his leaves. No doubt about him needing some kind of help.

. . . DANCE IN THE END ZONE

Thighs pounding like pistons, Ted worked the StairMaster, feeling the burn. Had me meet him at the Residents Club, Harbour Square, bring him the envelope of cash, told me to bring my sweats. Looking at me stepping on the next machine, he checked around, made sure nobody was within earshot. Told me Mateo Cruz had his crew prepping the cars, the ones just bought at auction, shipping them from Poughkeepsie. Welding the cells in place, packing them with Uzis. Pistols in sealed bags in the gas tanks.

"Yeah, so where they crossing?"

"You'll know when you get down there."

"One bit at a time, huh?"

"Yeah. And take Vick along, want the two of you riding shotgun, both keeping an eye."

"Want to run it by me, what went wrong last time?"

"Shit that can't go wrong again." Giving me the short strokes of what went down at the Beamsville scales, Bucky Showalter getting jumped. "Reason I want both of you going." He stepped off the machine, wiping a towel at the sweat. "Gonna fill the showroom by end of the week.

Everybody getting what they want." Slinging the towel around his neck, saying, "Let's grab a schwitz. Make you feel like a million."

Following him to the lockers, peeling off my sweats and undershirt, tossing them in the gym bag, wrapping myself in a towel, I stepped in the sauna. Hit by a wall of heat and steam, I took the bottom bench, Ted going to the top, saying, "Toss some water, will you?"

Reaching the bucket, I poured, the water hissing on the stones. Not liking the way this was going, being kept in the dark, knowing he was holding back.

"Toss some more," Ted said, leaning back, breathing deep, telling me again there'd be another envelope for each of us when we got back.

If we got back.

Randy Hooper and Pony White stepped from the rig, Hooper Towing in white serifs in black outline down the orange sides. A black Suburban sat parked by a meter, its windows tinted. Donning the work gloves, wearing coveralls, name on the pocket, Pony White hauled the chain off the back, taking his time, checking out the big Chevy's front end. Standing up on the curb, Randy lit a smoke. Waiting.

First to see the two Bent Boys coming from X Dales, crossing Carlingview. The strip club open at noon, another peeler pub slopping up an all-you-can-eat buffet. Dirty Leg and Blue Eyes looking around as they stepped into the street, dodging the daytime traffic.

"Don't even think about it, my man," Blue Eyes said, stepping close to Pony, arms loose at his sides. Pony holding the chain in both hands.

"District contract," Randy said, leaning on the meter, pointing to its red flag.

"You kidding, right?"

"City takes a dim view. Don't feed the meter, you get towed. How it works."

"So you just hook up a man's ride while he's standing here, uh?" Blue Eyes smiling.

"The good news, you get her back when you pay the fine."

"Somebody gonna be paying, that part's sure enough," Blue Eyes said.

Randy grinned. "I wanted to hook up your ride, would've done it while you were in catching your daytime titty." Stepping to the back of the tow truck, he lifted an oily tarp, just enough so they could see what was under it.

Blue Eyes and Dirty Leg glancing at the Uzi, then at each other.

Blue Eyes saying, "Gonna try and sell us something we already paid for, huh?" Still easy, still smiling.

"Ask me, you boys are having trouble getting deliveries."

"Way it looks, uh? And we deal with you, then you see an end to our troubles, I right?"

"You got it." Randy wrapped the Uzi, offering it to Blue Eyes.

"And how much we be paying for what's already ours?" Blue Eyes looking around, then taking the gun.

"What's yours is yours. Just want to show you there's a better way."

"You got the floor, my man."

"Give me a number, I call you here tonight, name a place where we hand them over."

"Just like that?"

"Just like that."

Blue Eyes giving him a number, Randy turned and got in the passenger side. Tossing the chain in the back, Pony smiled at Dirty Leg, backed to the driver's door and climbed behind the wheel, starting up the tow truck. Blue Eyes and Dirty Leg watching them drive off, then looking at each other.

Blue Eyes saying, "Lot of crazy fuckers in this town."

Dirty Leg nodding.

"If it wasn't for the house . . ." Ann had let her words hang, got out and slammed the Gran Fury's door, walking into the library for her shift. Pissed on account I didn't tell her about the showroom getting shot up, skirted around the fight at Valencia's and was sketchy about where the rest of the cash for the house had come from. I told her I didn't want her worried, sweating the details, but she wasn't buying it.

Sitting under the Chuvalo, I replaced the cord on the phone with the new one I picked up at Canadian Tire, plugged it in and listened for dial tone.

Vick came up the steps. Shutting the door, he sat in the spare chair, taking out a pack of smokes, tapping one out, saying, "Been thinking, maybe we ought to bail."

"How you mean, bail?"

"Got to know we're being played, right? The man hands us some money, tells us to take a ride, not telling us what's what, where we're going."

"Just being careful."

"Figuring us for two ex-cons too dumb to know better."

He fished in a pocket for his matches. "Ask me, we're being played from both ends."

"Both ends?"

Vick shrugged, stuck the smoke in his mouth, found a match and lit up. Another guy not talking.

"We bail, then what? Work the hair thing?"

"Least nobody'll be shooting at us." Vick puffed, blowing a stream of smoke at the ceiling.

"Something you're not saying?"

"Saying I'm sick of living on maybes and Arby's, same as you. Desperation's been jerking my chain, money trouble messing my head. You got no fucking idea."

"Really think I been riding high?" I said.

Quiet in the room, just the gurgle of the fountain. Vick tossing in another wooden match.

"Do what you want, but I'm making this run," I said.

He puffed, flicking ashes in my fountain, looking unsure.

... SHIT BEFALLS US

Recent rains washed the sky smogless, a brilliant blue past the CN Tower, rush hour on the Gardiner easing. I reached the shades off the dash, the meeting at the downtown Commerce branch had gone better than expected. With the seller taking back a small second, the assistant manager said he could approve the first, telling me it would take a day or two to get it all approved. Ted's letter of employment, with fudged projected earnings, and the cash I'd scraped together making the difference. I knew guys in the Don that waded through deeper shit than this every day. Kept telling myself that, but my hands were sweating on the wheel, and I had that feeling like I was being choked again.

Ann was off to the paint store, getting more paint chips and signing out wallpaper books, looking for the perfect bunny border, wanted me to like it, too.

Traffic was light past the Exhibition grounds, and I was thinking about this ride to Poughkeepsie. I guess I drifted into the next lane, the blaring horn making me jerk back into my lane. Looking over at the grey van — Bundy and Egg in the next lane. Bundy smiling and showing the pruners, Egg swerving and crowding my lane. Stupid cross bobbing from the mirror.

Pulling to the right, I tromped on the brakes, heard the screeching just as a Taurus plowed my rear end, shoving me against the guardrail, scraping the side. More honking and crunching metal, cars behind me swerving in a crazy sheet-metal ballet, the Taurus flipped on its side, instant four-lane pileup, plugging up the Gardiner. Stepping on the gas got me clear.

The grey van pulled a length ahead, Bundy rolling down his window.

I steered around a pickup ahead. Less traffic as I reached under my seat for the Ruger. Rolling down the window, I aimed with my left hand, seeing the hole Ted shot in their door, thinking I'd add a couple of my own.

A bottle with a burning rag stuffed in the top came out their passenger window, and I swerved right, dropping the pistol, scraping the guardrail again, losing the right mirror, the cocktail bursting on the tarmac as I flew past.

Taking the clear passing lane, Egg got around a junk man's truck. GOT JUNK lettered large and yellow across the tailgate, the bed heaped with the guts from a house demo. The old man behind the wheel banged on his horn, fighting for control.

I tried passing on the right, Egg cutting in front of the junk man, making him swerve my way, his rusted tailgate dropping down. An avalanche of debris rained across the lanes, junk smashing and bouncing and rolling. The old man swerved, lath flying off the back, chunks of drywall, shingles, strapping.

Boards bounced off my grill, tires crunching over shit. Dropping back, I missed a set of louvers. A toilet basin exploded, copper pipe bounced like pasta across the lanes. With a quick heel-toe, I did a slalom move. Debris flying up and slapping the windshield.

Thud. Thud. Thud.

Flooring the Gran Fury past the junk truck, looking through the spidered windshield, I saw the Jameson exit up ahead. The grey van cutting across the lanes, forcing me to jerk right again, my rocker striking more guardrail, metal crumpling. GOT JUNK plowed into their side and sent the grey van rolling onto its roof.

Fighting the drag, I oversteered and lost control and spun one-eighty, my shades flipping from my face. Screeching and slamming against the rail.

GOT JUNK skidded to a stop. Upside down in the van, Bundy tried kicking at the windshield. Egg not moving.

No cars came from behind me, must have been a hell of a pileup. That and GOT JUNK's load. Heart pounding, I cranked the key and got the engine to cough to life. Turning the Gran Fury around, I heard the sound of distant sirens. Working the column shift, I rolled down the ramp, a scraping sound coming from underneath. Hoping nobody got my plate, knowing I had to dump the car, call it in stolen. Taking the Jameson exit, across Queen and up Roncesvalles, a couple kids pointing at my ride, dragging the sparking bumper.

... RIPPLE

The clerk had the AM set to CHUM, Springsteen filling the liquor store, the twang of the Boss rising over the sirens out on the expressway. Taking a box of burgundy from a rack, going to the cash, I set it on the counter, my whole body still shaking.

Looking me over, the clerk seemed to have his doubts about selling booze to a crazy. Looked at me like he figured I was well over twenty-one and probably already had a mother; top of that, there was no telltale smell and no slurred words. And then there was the golden rule of liquor-store clerks: avoid any kind of shit that could lead to getting shot. He took my twenty and made the necessary change. Wishing me a good day, he waited on the next customer in line. All with a smile.

I heard another siren en route to the Gardiner pileup. Setting the wine box on top of the pay phone at the corner of the strip of stores, I took out a handful of change, fished out a quarter, called to let Ted know the Gran Fury wasn't going to make the ride to Poughkeepsie, waiting for him to pick up. Battered and beaten, I had left it parked down a side street, bleeding out antifreeze.

... TWO-TIME LOSERS

Standing at the window of his condo, Ted Bracey felt the sun coming through the glass, but there was an autumn cool about it. Still boats out on the lake, though; Ted thinking he'd take out the Sea Ray. Reaching for the phone, he answered, appraising Ginger wiggling into her panties. Man, that body. Back in the day, he would have taken the receiver off the hook and done her a couple more times. This girl half his age, giving him all the push-back he could handle. Ted hoping to be around long enough to ask for her again. Ginger making him forget the quicksand of shit he stood at the brink of. Maybe next time, he'd take her out in the boat.

It was Jeff calling from a pay phone, an edge to his voice. Ted saying, "What's up?"

●

I explained the situation. "Fuckers bounced me into the guardrail, more than once."

"Sure it was the same guys?" Ted said, like he didn't

believe these guys were back for more after he'd put a round through their door.

"No way I'll make Poughkeepsie in that." I steadied the box of wine on top of the phone box, wanting to tap it.

He told me to leave the car. "Get your ass in a cab and pay cash, leave a tip big enough so the guy forgets your face." Said he'd take care of calling it in stolen.

●

Ted watched Ginger wiggle into her skirt, snap on her bra, slip on her heels, button her blouse. Blowing him a kiss, she caught her bag by the strap. Flipping her red hair, she said, "See you around, Teddy," letting herself out.

That hair. That skin. Ted thinking there were no lips, no legs, nothing like that in any House of Corrections, not on this God's green Earth. No matter what you paid for it.

●

Hanging up, I steadied the box, flipped open the phone directory on the chain, found the listing for taxis, stuck in my last quarter, made the call. Grabbing the box, I went and waited by the curb.

Remembering I hadn't called Penny back, the woman waiting to hear from me, needing to get her hands on the certified check. First call I'd make when I got home. Sitting on the box of burgundy at the curb, I wrung my hands together, couldn't get rid of the tingling, telling myself to hang in there, just be another day or two. Make the run to Poughkeepsie, get the cars across the border, get the deed to the place, make peace with Ann. Getting up, I waved at the yellow cab slowing.

. . . DOWNSTROKE

I sat at the table, the box on top of it with the spigot hanging over the side, working on my second glass. Ann watched like she was getting a temperature read, the dishwasher chugging through its last rinse cycle.

"I got flattened boxes," she said, pouring herself a glass. "Went to that Stor-All place," she said, taking a sip.

"Uh huh."

"Can't believe the junk we got in the crawl space and out in the garage, all your widowed socks in the drawer, half with holes."

"Uh huh."

"Promised to darn them. Remember?"

Looking at her, seeing her mouth moving, not really hearing the words.

"You listening, Jeff?" Ann saying if I clipped my toenails once in a while . . . Putting her hands on her hips, she stared until I looked up.

"Not listening again."

"Been that kind of day, Ann," I said, working my thumbnail under the chipped Formica. Taking a swallow, I held the glass under the spigot and topped it. The tingling in my fingers was gone now.

Ann saying she spent the afternoon finalizing the paint chips: Silver Lining for the entry hall, Gingersnap for the kitchen, a William Morris paper pattern for the powder room. Gave up searching for a bunny border. Looking at me, she frowned and said, "Never going to change, is it?"

"Listening, Ann. Silver Lining for the entry." I looked at her.

"Ask myself every day why I stick around. Know what it means, Jeff, me thinking that way?"

"Means you're gonna start." Not sure why I said it, I tipped up the glass, felt good going down. "Look, Ann —"

"Uh uhn. Gonna let me finish."

"You got to start?"

"Not going to start, Jeff. Going to finish."

"Look, Ann. We're nearly there. Getting things worked out. Getting Penny the check —"

"Oh . . ." Ann putting on the theatrics again, slapping a palm to her forehead, saying, "Nearly forgot, she called." Her eyes drilling into me.

"Penny?"

"Told me about the clause you stuck in, one we didn't talk about, wanting the seller to fix the statue."

"Right, the fountain. Yeah, a good idea, buy us some time till the bank comes through."

"She warned us, go in clean with no clauses."

"Like I said, Ann, just buying some time."

She refilled her glass, saying, "You went to the bank, right?"

"Told you I did. Where I just was, spent half the afternoon. What's your problem?"

"While you were doing, whatever, she called, Penny, telling me we lost it . . ."

"What?"

"Should say you lost it . . . over your cement cock." Tears rolled as she filled in the rest. Penny had called while I was playing demolition derby on the Gardiner, told Ann the sellers were going with the other offer, it coming in clean with no conditions. Nothing more she could do.

The dishwasher finished its rinse cycle and ground to a stop, sounded like a death rattle. Downing half her glass in a swallow, Ann poured some more, pulling open the machine's door. She leaned her head into the escaping steam of the Norge, breathing deep, saying, "Ah, a day at the spa."

The tingling was back in my hand.

... THE MADMAN'S MOSH

The garage was dim under the fluorescent tube above the workbench, cobwebs hanging from the mounting chains. Ann pounded nails into a two-by-four. Some she sank, some she bent, the board looking like a pincushion. Paint cans and hand tools hopped on the bench as she struck. She grabbed a fistful more nails from the Beaver Lumber bag. Driving the hammer down through the wine fog, swearing like a chant . . .

Fuck.

Fuck.

Fuck.

Patching the tears in my suit with packing tape, doing it in the bedroom, applying it from the inside to hide the rips, I heard the banging and went to the garage door, watching. Ann giving up on the Zen, looking in need of a white jacket with the long sleeves, due for some cognitive-behavioral therapy. Tears streamed down her cheeks. Catching my shadow, she looked over, saying, "Should've listened to Deb. Damned house was a pipe dream, always was."

"Come on Ann, how's this helping? Do your breathing, relieve some stress or something."

"I am relieving stress." Gripping the hammer like she might attack.

"How about a cup of tea. I'll make it?"

"Know what I don't need, don't need you telling me what I need."

"There'll be other places."

"You hear the one about the ex-con walks into a bank, tries to get a loan." Taking the hammer like a microphone, doing another one of her Robin Leach bits, saying, "Sure, Mr. Nichols, how much you need?"

"A cash offer came in, and they went with it. Simple. Not my fault."

"Goddamn turned my life to crap with your bullshit promises, keeping me in the dark. Same way it always turns out." Holding a nail, she slammed the hammer down.

"Can't deal with you like this." I said I had a bag to pack. Had to get my mind on Poughkeepsie. Ted putting Vick and me on a plane, the flight leaving at nine in the morning.

I left her slamming the hammer, and she must have missed, striking her hand.

Howling.

I went back to the door in time to see her do the madman's dance of pain, clamping the hand between her knees, jumping and glaring at me and gritting her teeth.

"You okay?"

All I got was a low growl. Taking a step like she might attack, she slipped on the oil stain. Whirling her arms, she lost her balance and went down hard, the hammer pinging off the work bench.

Going to her, I swept the hammer away with my foot, tried to help her up, but she pushed me off, yelling, "Get away from me!"

Folding the suit, the bite marks on the trousers and a dried crust of slobber on the sleeve, I laid it in the suitcase. Coming in, composed now, Ann sat at the end of the bed, looking at her thumbnail turning black.

"Bet it hurts, huh?"

"I don't know you," she said, dumping the suitcase on the floor, my clothes and toiletries ending in a heap.

I looked down at it, and she said, "This one's mine." Going to the dresser, she went about filling it with her stuff. "Wouldn't listen to me, you and your fucked-up job."

"If it were up to you, I'd be slopping chili in bowls, serving it with saltines, the lunch counter at Kresge's or someplace."

"Keep it up, Jeff, even they won't take you." She sat for a moment, saying, "You know, living with Dale beat this. Worst he ever did was slap me around once in a while."

"That what you want, me slapping you around?"

"Try it." Her eyes wide and crazy. I'd seen that look in the Don often enough to know to keep quiet.

Pressing down the overstuffed case, she zipped it up

and stalked down the hall and out the door, slamming it behind her.

Swiped my foot at my pile of clothes, saw a fresh hole in my sock, and I got to thinking of Vick's desk lighter, how easy it would be to just torch the place. After a while, I went to the closet and dug around in back, seeing if there was some kind of bag I could pack my stuff in. Telling myself she'd be here when I got back, at least by the time her thumbnail healed.

... FRIENDLY SKIES

Easing into the coach seat, I stared out at the grey, replaying the scene with Ann, telling myself again she'd be there when I got back from Poughkeepsie. Out the window, the Oshawa ground crew buzzed around. The pilot coming on the intercom, warning of some turbulence on the way to Westchester, mentioning the stopover in Philadelphia.

Pulling down his armrest, Vick was talking about Jackie nailing down an exclusive contract with her South American inventor, called to tell him last night. Said we should get out of this thing with Ted after hearing what happened to me on the Gardiner. Then he feigned fumble-fingers, letting the stewardess buckle him in, listening to her explain about the new audio player. Vick asking her if this tub had a toilet, looked to where she pointed, shifting his hip so she could get at the buckle, making a joke about the mile-high club.

Straight blonde bob with the bangs falling over her eyes. A nice scent and freckles dotting the top of her cleavage. Her name tag said she was Melodie. She said he'd obviously never seen the size of the can in one of these tubs, giving him a wink, leaving him with, "There you go, sir."

Elbowing me, he guessed her accent came from down under, watching her walk the aisle toward the cockpit, hips sweeping under the skirt. Melodie getting the other passengers settled.

"Nice, uh?" Pointing to her. "Sense of humor, too."

"Yeah, nice." I was back to staring out the window, past the black turboprop, watching the ground crew working.

"Sure make a man forget the shit he's wading in." Vick watched her aid an elderly passenger, stowing a bag under the seat.

"Think you need some kind of priority, get your life straight."

"Yeah, ask me, you sound like you need to get laid." Reaching in his jacket pocket, he pulled out a pamphlet, smoothed it, saying, "No idea why I'm doing this, but here."

I took it, the picture of a guy singing.

"Guy me and Archie met at the trade show, name's Conway Forbes." Vick pointing to the logo, saying, "Guy can teach anybody to sing."

I pulled the pamphlet open, a picture of the same guy singing to an auditorium of onlookers.

"Conway's looking to get himself on the fast track. Figured with the courses you took inside — I don't know — thought it might be right up your alley."

"Trying to help me, huh?" Not sure the weekend entrepreneurship program and two weeks of learning to write business plans would help.

"Take it how you want. You know, by the time you see this ain't working out, always good to have a backup."

"Making this work."

"Every seminar this guy Conway fills the joint, gets people singing like canaries. People buying his cassettes, walking away happy, saying they had no idea they could sing like that."

"So, this is you . . . extending an olive branch, huh?"

"Call it what you want, but when this car deal goes bust . . ."

I handed the pamphlet back, saying, "Maybe get this guy to train your Elvis stable."

"Up yours." Tucking it in the seat-back pocket, he looked like he wanted to add to my bruises, then glanced back up the aisle, watching Melodie settle the last of the passengers.

"Alright, sorry," I said. "Guess maybe we both been played."

"Blind man can see that."

"That why you ratted the route to Randy?" I looked at him.

He glanced away, then said, "Randy's not a guy who gives a man a lot of options."

We sat quiet, then I reached for the pamphlet again and said, "So, this Conway guy's got some cash, huh?"

Vick grinned. "You're fucking welcome."

The seat belt warning chimed on, and the twin props started spinning.

"They say this is the worst part," he said, looking past me out the window.

"What's that?"

"Mechanical failure. Happens, it'll be just after takeoff. The wheels come off the ground, and . . ." He made a diving motion with his hand.

"Man, you're the life of the party, you know it?" Ripping into the cellophane, I shook out the cheap headphones and plugged in the prongs, getting some Miles Davis, feeling the jet vibrate, the noise of the props cutting into his *Blue Period*.

Melodie came back up the aisle, doing a final seat belt check. Vick letting her snap his buckle again, like he couldn't do it. Then he tapped my arm, saying, "You ever think about it?"

"What?

"Ending it."

I pulled out the buds.

"After the wife left, the second one, I did, thought about it, now and then. Got over it, then after the cardboard fire and landing in the Don. Thought about it a lot. The tunnel, the white light, what's on the other side, the shit you read, you know . . ."

"That's damned unhealthy thinking, Vick."

"Yeah, well, that was then."

"Doing it like how, pills?"

"Always had trouble swallowing stuff like that. Even with the water. Always end up chewing them, always tastes like shit."

"How about hanging, shooting?"

"Painful, violent . . ." Vick started to smile.

"Jumping off a ledge, let me guess," I said. "Got a thing about heights?"

"Get queasy just thinking it." Vick grinned and was watching Melodie take her position up the aisle, ready for the safety demonstration, pointing out the exits to the passengers.

"Could just annoy somebody enough, get them doing it for you."

Demonstrating how to inflate a life preserver found under the seat, Melodie put her mouth on the tube, then showed the oxygen mask.

Nodding and pointing to her, Vick said, "Asphyxiation, now there's the way to go."

"Well, glad that's resolved." Putting the buds back in my ears, I turned up the jazz and looked back out the window, the plane starting to taxi, the engines droning louder, drowning out Miles and his trumpet.

. . . POUGHKEEPSIE SHUFFLE

The peaks of Huntersfield gave way to the green valleys, giving way to low-level buildings. Napping with my head against the window after the layover in Philly, two hours of waiting and downing soft pretzels and cheesesteaks, I woke looking out with a stiff neck, feeling bloated, the twin-engine making its final descent to Dutchess County.

Vick was talking local geography, Melodie leaning and pointing out the Hudson River running past the city. Vick asking what she was doing later, inviting her out for drinks, hearing her say sorry, she was making a return flight. Told him some other time maybe and left him with a smile.

Getting our bags from the carousel, we made our way past arrivals. Over by the exit, a tall, thin guy stood watching, coming over like he guessed who we were. Introducing himself as Mateo Cruz, he shook our hands. Smiling, he led us out to his car, a Continental with the grill and flip-up lights. Lighting a smoke by the doors, Vick glanced around one more time for Melodie.

Warding off a pair of taxi hustlers with a look, Mateo popped the trunk, the two of us dropping in our bags.

Mateo wheeled his way onto the Number 9, heading for Poughkeepsie, pointing out the Walkway Over the Hudson, telling us how the Dutch side of his ancestry bought this place from the Indians, throwing around names like Van den Bogaert, the first guy who made it with Mateo's maternal Spanish side. Mateo telling us most of these folks now worked for IBM. Throwing in that it used to be home to the Smith Brothers Cough Drops factory, the stuff working magic on a sore throat. Pointing out the spire of the First Presbyterian over some rooftops, place he went Sunday mornings.

"Got a decent place to eat?" Vick said.

"Main drag's nothing but a line of cafes, any one worth checking out."

Not interested in food right then, I asked about the cars. Looking at me, Mateo said his guys were detailing the last ones, be ready to go tomorrow. Telling us he had us booked in a nice place, the Hudson Inn.

"So, you and Ted figure where we're crossing?" Vick said.

"Ted's gonna call, let you know," Mateo told him.

"When's that?"

"When you need to know."

. . . PACT MAN

The detail shop had graffiti scribbled down its exposed cinder block side. Bars on the windows and a line of the cars from the auction out back. Mateo pointed out a Cimarron with the fake cabrio roof, the only one not being detailed.

"You boys get to drive back in the Caddy."

"Call that a Caddy?" Vick said, looking inside the shop, saying he'd take the Cutlass or the Tempest up on the hoists, a couple of Mateo's guys in coveralls getting them ready. I was thinking, this from the man with a junkyard Jag in his garage.

"Yeah, what do you normally drive?" Mateo said.

"Jag, xj in racing green, but, that's beside the point."

Not impressed, Mateo explained the Caddy wasn't strapped, meaning with guns. Walking under the hoist on the left, he pointed to the cells welded under the Cutlass. Could hardly see them, even knowing where they were. Mateo promised his cells were good enough to fool any border inspection, the guys with their sniffer dogs, holding their mirrors underneath and checking. A half dozen Uzis, converted and full auto, strapped under each one. The Bent Boys shelling out two Gs apiece.

Giving a dirty look at the Cimarron on the way out, Vick said GM should've called it the Hubris, or the Cavillac, the thing nothing but a trimmed-up Cavalier.

Leading us from the garage, Mateo said he'd called ahead for a table at a place called the Dutchess, the three of us sitting over Heineken and Bols, me gaining my appetite back. Following drinks with a thick pea soup with sausage, with a name I couldn't pronounce, Vick going for a stew called hachée, the three of us downing a couple bottles of cabernet. After we wolfed down dinner, the waiter came with apple pie, best I ever had.

Between sips of after-dinner drinks, Vick said again he didn't like not knowing where we were crossing.

"Know when you need to know," Mateo said again. "Main thing's to get through." Waving for the waiter, he ordered another round, saying, "May as well kick back, boys, take it easy." Talking some more folklore about this ghost that rolled its flaming head down a set of stairs, a story that had spooked the locals for decades. Pointing up the street, where it was supposed to happen. Mateo saying we were sitting maybe fifty miles from Sleepy Hollow, asked if we knew about the headless horseman.

"Read about it when I was like twelve." Vick shrugged, sinking the contents of his glass, saying, "How about we forget the ghost stories, man, no offense, but you got any women in this town?"

Mateo saying it was a quiet family place, the reason they picked it for the detail shop.

"Least the vino's decent," Vick said, looking around for the waiter.

"You're drinking pear brandy," Mateo said, looking over at me, shaking his head, laughing. I shrugged. All I knew, it beat the hell out of the stuff that came in a box with a spigot.

"The Hudson's known for its fruit brandies and cordials."

"Yeah, but, no women," Vick said.

After a couple more rounds, we followed him to a place a few doors up called the Horseman's Hollow, a few married couples slow-dancing on a flagstone floor to some Juice Newton number coming from a Wurlitzer. Sitting out back in Adirondack chairs overlooking the Hudson, we let more drinks slide down. Manicured lawn with a hedgerow out back, the sun dropping beyond the distant trees, putting everything in silhouette. The gathering dusk brought an owl's hoot above the chorus of crickets. A light breeze blew from the north.

Mateo ordered a final round, and I handed out the Cubans I had in the top pocket of my jacket, snuck them across.

Thanking me for the smoke, Mateo said he was hoping things were going to roll smooth this trip. Told us the driver, Bucky, had a sawed-off pump and a couple handguns for us.

"Hell of a thing, the cars getting jacked like that," Vick said.

"Yeah, sometimes the shit rolls sideways," Mateo said, "but all that's in the rearview. Debt's been squared. We got customers waiting, plus we got you boys riding shotgun, make sure it gets there."

A waiter in white came out with a tray, setting it down, pouring strong coffee into china cups, passing them around. I didn't remember anybody ordering it.

Puffing on his cigar, Mateo paid the check, said he'd drop off the Caddy, that he'd call our room in the morning before the truck headed out.

"And let us know where we're crossing," Vick said.

. . . FLYING HIGH, MOANING LOW

Just gone midnight, the two of us staggered into the lobby of the Hudson Inn. A drowsy-looking desk clerk roused to our echoing footsteps on the travertine, the two of us laughing about something. Vick tugged my sleeve, pulled me past the elevators, making for the Trafalgar Bar. Vick still going on about Ted and Mateo not showing any trust.

"On account you been selling them out."

"Like I had a choice," he said.

"You always got a choice, man."

"Would have quit, you know it, thrown in with Jackie fresh out of the Don if Randy hadn't been in the picture."

"Guy's bad news, that's for sure."

"You got no idea, man." Talking through the booze fog, Vick told me about the time Randy rained a shitstorm on this dude named Brother Louie. "Guy ran this shop called Domingo's or something in Kensington Market. You know the place?"

"Kensington, yeah, sure."

"Story goes Randy stops by to collect on a poker debt or some shit Brother Louie'd been ducking him on. Anyway, one thing leads to another, and Louie says he won't pay on account of Randy cheating. Cheating. Fuck. 'Course Randy takes a swipe at him, and Louie sets his Portu-guys on him."

"Portu-guys, huh?"

"Yeah, bunch of them beating on Randy and tossing him out back, dumping him on a crate of rotting food. Cabbage, think it was."

The booze had me laughing, trying to picture it.

"So he scrapes himself up, goes and gets Pony and Luther and some chains off the tow truck. Beats Brother Louie and his guys bloody, falling or running. Randy collects his dough, then sets a match to Domingo's. Burned it to the ground, cabbage and all."

"Like I said, the guy's bad news." I was looking at the dim lights of the bar, the walls painted dark, an old bartender in a striped shirt, polishing glasses. The only customers, a couple of women perched on bar stools, feigning conversation over watered drinks — both heavy on the makeup and light on the dress. Thinking about what Mateo said about there being nothing but families in town.

Base nature drew Vick to the bar. Not thinking about anything but the women smiling our way.

"I got to hand it to you . . ." I hooked his sleeve, trying to slow him down, saying I liked the way he played it with Mateo.

He was past hearing me, sizing up the women. Dark-haired, dark skinned, both putting out the signals. One with an hourglass build, the other taller, with hawkish looks, showing a beguiling nature.

"Bracey give you an expense account, credit card, something like that?" he said.

"You're kidding, right?"

Vick scraped back his chair, sat and lapped up that flesh, tanned and oiled. Perfume reaching our table.

"Got a couple more Cohibas up in the room," I said. "What say we grab a couple bottles, some ice, and head up? Got a big day coming."

"And pass this up? You going gay on me? All that time in the joint?" Vick wagged for the bartender, calling, "Cervezas, por favor."

The bartender giving him a look.

"Know we're in New York, right?" I said.

Vick called to him again, ordered a couple Buds in English, saying to me things were looking up on all fronts.

I glanced over at the bartender, silver hair with a big sweeping mustache, wiping a glass with his apron, going to a cooler, reaching in and pulling up a couple of bottles, the man's eyes held the look of someone who could rhyme off about a hundred places he'd rather be. Cracking them open, he shuffled over, setting them on the table.

"And whatever the ladies are having," Vick said to him, smiling and angling his chair toward the women. "Beunas noches, ladies." The lights behind the bar put them in silhouette, their features looking hard.

"From Canada, eh?" the tall one said, turning and leaning, cleavage jiggling.

Smiling at her, Vick sucked down half his beer.

Ann was the one who walked out, I said to myself, watching the women swivel toward us, the raised bar stools leaving little to the imagination. Breasts pushed up, rifts of pleasure, oiled legs under short skirts, letting our eyes go where they wanted. That part was free.

Tipping back the rest of his beer, Vick cupped a hand to his mouth and squelched a burp, flipping that mental coin. Leaning close, saying to me, he'd go for the tall one first, calling the other one Ample.

"Gonna pass, but you go ahead," I said.

"What, you want the other one?"

"Take 'em both, Ample, too, if you want."

"A man's got needs, even you, am I right?"

"Not tonight."

I guessed if it wasn't for all the booze, he'd last about minute with either one. Vick sitting there with the numb grin of a drunken fool, the tall one zeroing in on him. Ample swiveled to me. I put up a hand, stopping her. She looked at me like she wasn't sure if I was arrogant or impotent or just too plastered.

Vick was telling them we were with a car outfit, calling us execs here on business, turning to me and asking, in what he thought was a low voice, if I was packing.

"Like a gun?"

"No, protection, man." Vick leaned close, saying he only brought a couple rubbers, packing light this trip.

The bartender came and set a second round on the table.

"Ask me, they probably got that covered," I said, watching the bartender set a couple more watered glasses on the bar in front of the women. The first ones still untouched.

Taking Vick's twenty, the bartender left, the look on his face saying this was the same old bullshit prelude to debauchery. Something he'd probably seen far too many times.

Sipping, Vick held his wallet low and checked his cash, both women eyeing him, the tall one saying half and half was a hundred.

"Half and half, huh?" Vick pulling out five twenties. "Was thinking more like double double."

"Each," she said.

Vick looking confused.

"Put that away," I told him. "Gonna get us busted?"

"By who?" He glanced around, saying to me, "Calm the fuck down, man. Place is empty. You wanna blow this for me?"

"Really think you got to work that hard here, huh?" I said.

"Just a little consideration, okay, all I ask. All that time locked up in that hellhole, I'm making up for it. Let's go double double." Vick counted out more twenties, the tall one leaning close, letting him make a deposit in the bank of cleavage. Letting him touch a finger to the smooth skin, Vick slipping in half the bills, repeating the process with the one he called Ample, saying to me, "Ask me, you need this more than me."

Probably right. I started on the second Bud, the beer near room temperature, giving it an off taste.

"Last time was . . ." Vick thinking out loud. "Night of Ted's party. Same time you were getting your ass kicked."

Smiling at Ample, I looked around the empty bar, part of me thinking what the hell, the other half thinking of Ann.

Downing his beer, Vick was out of his chair, tapping a cigarette from a pack, flaring a wooden match on his thumbnail, offering the pack around.

Taking a smoke, the tall one let Vick light her up, one hand holding back her hair, the other cupped over his, lips in an O. Blowing out his match, she thanked him, putting a hand to his chest, feeling his beating heart, looking at him like the rest of the money in his wallet was already hers, saying to him, "Double double, huh?"

"You betcha." Hooking his arm in hers, Vick guided her for the elevator, saying Archie was sure missing out on some good times.

Yeah, just what we needed, a greasy Elvis in flip-flops, singing lines from the Big E's songs.

Coming and sitting next to me, Ample pursed her lips and leaned near my ear, guiding my hand to her thigh, guessing she knew what that did to a man. Then leading me out of the bar and over to the elevator.

Vick had both hands on the tall one, using his elbow to press the elevator button.

Taking my hand back, I pointed to my ring finger, saying something about the old ball and chain.

Ample tapped a plastic nail against her own wedding band, shrugging, saying what did it matter. Taking my hand with the one with the ring on it, she set it back on her thigh, higher this time.

Still jamming his elbow at the elevator button, Vick worked his hands like he was kneading dough, told the tall woman his name, asking hers.

"Miss Right," she said, pointing over to Ample, saying, "and Miss Right Now."

Leaning close, Miss Right Now wet her lips, saying to me, "Your wife, she do this?" Leaning close, letting her tongue work my ear like she was sucking petrol up a hose. Had me up on my toes, feeling that through the booze fog. Original sin staring me in the face.

The elevator pinged, and the doors opened. Fingers pressing into Miss Right's flesh, Vick said to me, "Here's to too much bed and not enough sleep." Downing his Bud, he rolled the bottle on the elevator floor and was first on, pulling Miss Right in.

"Maybe I'll be there in a while," I said and pushed Miss Right Now in. The woman looking surprised as I stood there and watched it close, my morals winning over the booze, the three of them staring back at me.

... TURF

They had some words, Randy pissed on account of the missing Uzi. One of the three dozen Pony had stashed under the trailer at the towing yard was gone. Pony bitching how could it be his fault, no idea how somebody got in the yard last night with the three shepherd dogs running loose in the compound.

Randy got out of the passenger side, no time for that now, looking along the rail yards west of Union Station, a line of CN boxcars, the tower in the distance. Remembering his old man calling this place the hump yards. Pony checked his Colt and stuck it in a pocket, seeing the Lincoln pull up facing them, its headlights off. Getting from behind the wheel, he kept his eyes on the two Dreads stepping out, windows tinted all the way around. No way to tell if there were more inside. He kept a hand in his pocket.

Going around back of the tow truck, Randy held his hands in plain view, no point getting shot, these guys looking twitchy. The Dreads left both doors hanging open, the engine running, walking slow to the tow truck, both looking around.

Nobody smiling, nobody talking, keeping to the business. The taller one with a satchel loose at his side.

Lifting the Uzi from behind the tool box, Randy walked to the front and passed it over, the Dread with the satchel taking it, looking it over.

"What you asking?"

"Same as I said on the phone," Randy said. "Two Gs a pop."

The Dread snorted, saying, "Thought I heard that part wrong," then to the other one, "Man's got to be dreaming."

"Got three dozen just like it. Dream come true, I go and sell to the Bents. Boys be happy to pay what I'm asking, then go pointing them at you. Some might say we're not asking enough."

The Dreads looked at each other, the one handling the Uzi shrugged, saying, "Go high as a grand. Not the only guy in town selling." Tapping a hand against the satchel. "Cash. And we do it now, tonight."

Nobody saw the Suburban, with its lights off, rolling to a stop out front of the factory with the twin chimneys on top, the TD billboard on the roof. Three men climbing out, leaving the doors open, keeping low and fanning out, moving their way.

Randy, Pony and the Dreads stood facing each other, the Dread with the satchel saying he might go as high as twelve bills. "Get the coil on the spot, if you got 'em with you?"

The first bullet caught him high and spun him. Surprised look on his face, mouth flopping open. Raising the Uzi, he pressed the trigger on an empty clip. Tossing it aside, he jackrabbit-jumped along the tracks, grabbing his pistol and firing at the Suburban.

Diving for gravel, Randy and Pony crawled over the tracks to the tow truck, bullets whizzing overhead, punching into the truck's body. The second Dread was yelling and firing, making his way for the Lincoln. A burst of auto-fire taking him down. Muzzle flash showing from the Bent Boys' guns.

Getting in and jabbing the key in the ignition, Randy shoved the stick, more bullets tearing into the truck, pinging off the boom. Felt like somebody had kicked a nest of yellow jackets. Angry buzzing, lead pinging against the metal. Pony got in the other side, keeping low as Randy backed the hell out of there, swinging the rig around and driving off.

"Not your best fuckin' idea, man," Pony said to him, one hand on the dash, the other against the door, raising his head enough to look out the rear window, see if they were being chased.

•

Jerrel Bent stepped over the crisscrossing tracks, looked around to make sure there were no witnesses, straightened his suit jacket. Blue Eyes to his right, Dirty Leg going to the Dread lying closest to the Lincoln, the man writhing on the ground, moaning and bleeding from the back.

Tapping a foot at the satchel, pointing his pistol at the back of the man's head, Dirty Leg said something before firing a couple of rounds, picking up the Uzi, and checking the satchel, smiling at the cash inside. Blue Eyes going and checking the other man, coming back.

Turning back to the Suburban, Jerrel said he wasn't liking the way Randy Hooper did his double-dealing, said he took it personal.

. . . A TANGO OF LIMBS

The room was fusty from the night's sex and booze. I hung the *do not disturb* sign on the knob and shut the door, feeling the lines across my ass and back from spending the night on the lawn chair out by the pool. The only part of me that wasn't embossed was where the lump of my wallet spared me. Insect bites on both arms. Froze out there in the early morning damp, couldn't sleep on account of it, that and the thoughts of Ann leaving me. The only thing blanketing me was my suit jacket, that and the numbing hangover.

Sure wasn't the first thing I needed to see, Vick spread-eagled on the one bed, the bottoms of his feet black, the man laid out like a naked sacrifice, mouth open wide enough to drop a baseball into. Could see his fillings. Snoring on the inhale and exhale. The weasel at rest in its kinky-haired nest. I swatted at a mosquito, tried to nail it before it stuck its proboscis in me. God knows the toxic load the little beast held.

Looked like the hookers had plied their trade and split, the two of them not in the room. I swatted the air as I shuffled for the window, fighting the fuzziness, pulling the rod and the drape, the vista of the Hudson Valley a blur past the condensation on the inside of the glass. Working the latch, I yanked the window open.

"Rise and shine, Romeo." I tried not to look at Vick's slack weasel, my stomach feeling queasy enough.

His breath caught on a snore, he sputtered and stirred, eyes flickering, the snore turning to a groan.

Tapping the black foot dangling off the end of the bed with my shoe, I said, "Come on, man, get up."

Rolling on his side, he pulled a pillow over his head, told me to get lost, saying he felt like crap.

Going to the closet, I tossed my bag on the twin bed. "Let's get some coffee, get checked out of here." Opened the bag, getting out my change of clothes.

"Half hour's all I need."

"Get yourself some breakfast, you'll feel better," I said. "I'll drive the first shift, you can lay back." The Cimarron was supposed to be parked out front, Mateo sending one of his guys, the keys left at the front desk. Should get a call anytime, Mateo telling us where to cross.

Folding last night's shirt, I tucked it in the bag. Then I pressed down the packing tape over the tears in the jacket, it holding up pretty well.

"Was something, man." Vick gave a weak smile, trying to think of the hookers' names. "Those two couldn't get enough, was like my dick's magnetic, you know . . ."

"Think it, don't say it, okay? Come on, man, let's go." I tossed yesterday's socks in the bag.

Swinging a leg out, Vick hooked his hockey bag with his foot, inching it to him, saying, "Was me and Archie, we'd have switched and rode all night." Sitting up, he scanned around for his clothes. "Man, my fuckin' head's swimming. Getting old, uh?"

"Old, naw, just that blood rushing to your magnet." Going to the bathroom with my toothbrush in hand, I ran the water cold, getting a hit of mint in my mouth, brushing it around. Talking with the foam in my mouth, "And how about you put something on? You look like dried fruit."

"Barely see straight right now." Vick tried wiping the night from his eyes, slouched over the side of the bed and moaned, saying, "Good idea you do the driving, least till the border." Saying something about bringing a bag along to barf in.

He rummaged in the hockey bag, then looked in the desk and dresser drawers. Stuffing himself in his underpants, he dropped to his knees and lifted the bedskirt, checked underneath, then under my bed. Rising up, he went to the wall and looked behind the dresser, then looked in the bathroom, saying, "Fuck is it?" Vick put a hand to his temples.

"What?"

"My wallet." He checked behind the desk, then the dresser, tearing off the bedsheets, tossing the pillows at the corner of the room.

I came from the bathroom, swatted at the mosquito I thought was gone, watched Vick pull the nightstand drawer. He went to the closet, slapping a hand along the top shelf. Pulling on his jeans, he zipped up and cinched his belt, saying, "Didn't just walk out of here."

"Dumb shit falls asleep with hookers in the room. Surprise . . ."

"This is on you," he said. "Fucking first man down. Leaving me on my own, the two of them."

"You kidding me?"

"Fuck, just let me think," Vick said, rubbing a hand over his brow. "I was playing with Miss Right . . ." Fingers fondling the air, recreating the scene as he spoke. "The other one was fixing cc on ice." Looking to the minibar. "I took the bucket and went for more ice, down the hall, bent over, hoping nobody'd see me naked . . . Came back, the girls mixing drinks, and . . ."

"And . . . Mickeyed your drink."

Vick sat there, nodding like I must be right, saying, "Jesus, you can't trust nobody."

"Not even two hookers you find in a bar, huh? Sometimes, man, you're too stupid to live, you know that?"

"Yesterday it's good work, Vick, and have a Cohiba." Picking the Gideons from the nightstand drawer, he flung it at me, kicking the nightstand over. Dumping his hockey bag out on the bed, he searched again.

"How much they get?" I said.

"All of it."

"Money Ted gave you."

"Fuck." He turned to the digital clock between the twin beds, looking worried.

"He doesn't need to know."

"Not Ted I'm worried about."

"Money Randy gave you?"

He shrugged, saying, "Gonna have a bitch of a time explaining it, supposed to call him last night."

"Dragging me in with you . . ."

"Fuck y—"

My fist caught the side of his face, knocking him on the

bed, Vick blocking the next one. The two of us trading blows and grappling on the bed. Him punching up, me punching down. Neither of us able to put much into it.

The ringing phone stopped us both mid-punch, sagging bedsprings riding us to a stop.

Looking at the phone, I dropped my fist, saying, "Got to be Mateo."

"Maybe the chicks."

"Yeah, what, like a guilty conscience? Like, 'Here's your wallet'?"

Picking up the phone, he said, "Yeah?"

I could make out Jackie's tinny voice on the other end: "Vick, any idea how hard —"

Vick hung up, telling me it was just some guy selling shit, didn't know I knew it was Jackie. He got off the bed, tossing his stuff back in his hockey bag, saying, "Let's get that breakfast."

The phone rang again, and I beat him to it, answering. "Yeah?"

"Jeff?" Randy's voice. "What the hell, hanging up on Jackie?"

"Phone's iffy." I covered the receiver, mouthing to Vick, "Gonna kill you."

Throwing me the finger, he zipped up his bag.

"Expecting to hear from you boys," Randy said.

"Not me you want to talk to," I said.

"Then put Vick on."

Vick was shaking his head, like no way.

"He's gone for coffee."

"Where you crossing, Jeff?"

"Makes you think I'd —"

"Don't play me, Jeff."

"Not playing —"

Vick grabbed the receiver and yelled into the phone, "Kingston, 81 to Syracuse." Then he hung up and turned to me, held his hands out wide. "Want to hit me, go ahead. Nothing you can do'd be worse."

"You don't even know —"

Clapping his hands in the air in front of me — making me jump — he opened them, showing the squished mosquito in his palm.

. . . ASKING THE ANGELS

Three messages on the machine when Vick got home. A couple from Ted, another from Jackie. Taking his keys from the kitchen counter, he checked the lock on the sliding door. He topped up Tina's bowl with Dog Chow, put the bag back in the pantry. Ignoring the chow, Tina followed after him, Vick sliding the pistol under his shirt, so he could bend and slip on his shoes, scooping her up. The dog wriggled in his arms, tail wagging, licking his face, happy he was back, doing the man's-best-friend bit.

Telling her she was his best girl, asking if the lady next door took good care of her, he set her down and squeezed past the metal door into the garage, careful she didn't sneak through. Clicking on the light, he went to the Jag, running his hand along the liver-spotted rocker panel. Lighting a smoke and dragging on it, he yanked the creaking door and climbed in, looking around the interior, imaging her new, then cranking the key. Third try he got the engine coughing its fatigue, a couple more twists of the key and she sputtered to life. Pressing the pedal, he kept the revs above idle until she got used to the idea, idling on her own. Vick thinking of

227

that oneness with the open road, a feeling only a top-down touring driver knows, like soaring with the wind in his hair.

Faltering, the engine choked, kicked and gave up. Exhaust fumes rising to the roof beams. Coughing from the fumes, Vick pulled the hood latch and got out. Tina scratching at the other side of the kitchen door.

"Be a good girl, Tina —"

The garage door was pulled up from outside.

Vick stood looking at the three of them, the streetlamp casting them in shadow. Coming in. The door was pulled down.

"Know I got it wrong, but hear me out . . ." Vick going for the pistol.

. . . GETTING OFF

One of those grey October mornings, the boardwalk quiet for an early Saturday. Looked like a runaway in tatters with his matted hair and turned-up collar, shuffling up from the beach, the kid checking inside a trash barrel, a gull lifting off and crying about the intrusion. The kid looked like he'd come off an all-night blast, stumbling past us and brushing sand from his denim sleeve, smelling like he'd rolled in baitfish.

I fumbled for her hand, walking along the boards.

"Don't . . ." Ann snapped her hand away, saying, "Wanted to do this face to face, so there's no mistaking. It's over, Jeff." She waited, a group of tourists passing us armed with Nikons, a couple of them trying to make sense of a points-of-interest brochure, the runaway giving them directions, his hand coming out for change.

Maybe she had more to say, but the tears stopped her. Smiling as her eyes filling, she said, "All over a cement cock."

"There'll be other houses, Ann."

The tourists turned from the homeless kid, sensed our tension and watched us.

Turning off the boardwalk, Ann headed up toward Queen, shaking her head, saying, "Funny how I could see the flaws in the house, but not in us." Looking at me, she said again that we were done, her arms wrapped around herself.

Not sure why I didn't try to stop her, playing with the idea that she was right. Watching her go, I jingled the keys in my pocket, finally turning the other way and walking back to where I'd parked the Cimarron.

Driving along Queen, I stopped at a Tim Horton's, sat in there drinking coffee, hating my life, pretty sure I hated Toronto, too, thinking of other places I could go, start over, change my luck. Still thinking about it when I got back to our rental. Walking through the front door with the Ruger in my hand, I was swallowed by the emptiness. Ann had cleared most of her stuff while I was in Poughkeepsie, one of the chairs, the fountain off the hutch, her clothes all gone from the closet. The phone gave a hollow ring from the kitchen. Hoping it might be her, I picked it up, saying, "Yeah?"

"It's Vick." It was Jackie's voice.

"Know it's you, Jackie."

"Christ, Jeff. I'm saying it's Vick . . ."

"Look, Jackie, what we got to talk about?"

"He's gone."

"Gone where?" My first thought, he ducked out, leaving me in the shit he left behind.

"He's dead."

Felt like a slap.

"Cops think he asphyxiated himself, the way it looks, I don't know . . ."

I stared at the phone, heard her saying, "Near as they can tell, did it last night."

Vick's own words coming back, what he said on the turboprop, talking about offing himself. A call for help if ever there was one; and me, too wrapped up in my own crap to hear it.

"Cops figure he turned on that shitbox Jag. Maybe he meant to, or couldn't get out of there in time." Sounded like she was crying. "Warned him about that piece of shit," she said. "You were there."

"Yeah."

"Look, I know you two weren't close . . ." The sound of her blowing her nose, then talking over me as I tried to disagree, her saying, "Randy wants a word."

"Randy?"

"Yeah.

"Okay, put him on."

"Says to pick a time."

"Anything we got to say happens on the phone."

"Wants what's his, Jeff."

"I got nothing —"

"Two or two-thirty?"

"Got enough to deal with without your shit, Jackie."

"Tell you what, I'll put you down for two-thirty. Be at the car lot, have the door open. Save you driving all the way out here. And, Jeff?"

"Yeah?"

"Bring the Cadillac. Oh, and when you're done with Randy, might want to think about another town."

"Supposed to be a threat?"

"More of a warning. Cops are gonna find something at the car lot." The woman sounding like she was enjoying this.

"Find what?" When she didn't answer, I asked, "So why you warning me?" Not sure how much she knew.

"Not so much about the warning, Jeff, just want you to know who it was." Then she hung up.

I looked at the receiver, then threw it, watched it bounce around the linoleum, coming back, pulled by the coiled cord. Pulling the wine box from the cupboard, I poured the last of it into a juice glass, taking a long drink, hearing the dial tone coming from the receiver at my feet.

Wondering how much Vick told her, thinking about him and the last couple days. The hookers robbing him that night, the two of us not hearing from Mateo in the morning. Bucky Showalter coming by the Hudson Inn, told us he got word from Mateo last night, said we were crossing at the Peace Bridge. The two of us following Bucky's rig in the Cimarron. Both of us expecting to get hit. Making it to the AutoPark, getting the cars unloaded and parked on the lot. Last time I saw Vick.

. . . THE RAP

Unplugging the fountain, I drained it into the trash can, thinking of the stone fountain and the gelded cherub, splashing water across the desk, some getting under the Ruger I laid within easy reach. Stupid plastic fountain. I tossed it on the trash, its plug dangling on the floor. Setting the cigar box and cutter in the cardboard box, I went back to thinking of Vick on that flight, talking about ending it, and me not seeing it as a cry for help.

The buzz of the intercom had me jumping, my eyes on the office door. I'd locked the outer one. Got there early to grab my stuff, an hour ahead of the meet with Randy, the one I intended to avoid.

"Hey ya, Jeff." Randy's voice came over the intercom, sounding easy, like we were old friends.

"Yeah, hey Randy, came early, huh?" I reached the Ruger.

"So we're clear," he said. "I come up, and you're holding anything but my money, not gonna go so well for you, so we understand each other."

"Come on up and see." I clicked off, set the pistol on the desk, hearing his steps and watching the door open.

Shutting the door behind him, Randy put his own pistol on the desk and sat in the spare chair.

"Ever see him fight?" Looking at the Chuvalo behind me.

"Everybody asking me that."

"Hell of a thing. Old man took me down to the Gardens, him going against Ali. Nearly took it all the way. Ask me, fucking ref raised the wrong arm after the fifteen."

"Life's a bitch."

"So, where is it?"

"Whatever you want, I ain't got it. Maybe should've asked Vick."

"Gonna blame the dead guy?" Randy's eyes were black holes, his mouth was smiling, hand close to the pistol.

"Figured that was you, ripped off Ted's guns, Beamsville."

The corner of his mouth turned up.

"You do Vick, too?"

"That what you think?"

"It's what I'm asking."

"Vick sold you out, gave me the where and the when, was supposed to on the Poughkeepsie run, too, but, I guess you know that." Randy leaned on the desk, looking easy, saying, "But, don't go thinking bad of the man, didn't exactly give him much of an option. Same situation you're in now." Moving fast for a big man, he trapped my hand moving for the Ruger, pressing down as it went off, the bullet going through the wall.

Trying to jerk it free, I saw his other fist coming, the punch toppling me over the back of the chair. Head hitting the wall. Face on the floor, I got that copper taste in my mouth. Slow getting up, I dropped back into the chair, feeling my jaw, watching him dump the shells from the Ruger, pocketing them and tossing the pistol in the trash. His still on the desk.

"Paid good money for the hookers, supposed to keep you busy while we took the guns, went to your man Mateo's shop, right after you boys got done with your wining and dining. Trouble is, there were no guns, just cars up on a trailer."

"Talk to him, then."

"Tried that, had a nice talk while you two were hopping on the hookers. One thing for sure, you boys were having more fun than he was. I'll say this about Mateo, that man sure could keep his mouth shut, nothing coming out but crying and moaning, never said a word. Even with Pony drilling a hole through one knee cap, then the other. Guy wouldn't say shit about guns. Right to the end."

"They were in cells, hidden underneath."

"Yeah, like Beamsville, what everybody was supposed to think. Thing is, they weren't. Ted Bracey using you two like worms on a hook."

I heard footsteps come up the stairs, Pony White coming in, pistol in one hand, the drill in the other, shaking his head. Guess he'd been looking around out back.

Randy looked back at me. "Not at Vick's, not here, not at your place."

"You broke in my place?"

Randy saying, "So, where are they?"

"Already told you —" Saw the fist coming, knocking me into the wall. A hundred telephones ringing, neon dots exploding. And I was back on the floor.

Coming around the desk, Randy snagged my shirtfront,

propped me up against the wall, getting nose to nose, saying, "Tell me no again, and you and Vick'll be having a reunion."

Pony hit the trigger, spinning the drill bit, saying to Randy, "Let me give it a try." He started to move from the door, then said, "Shit!" Getting inside the office, tucking himself against the wall, sticking his head out enough to see the entrance. "Cops."

Randy tightening his grip, saying, "Shhh."

I pointed at my throat, couldn't breathe, Randy looking at me, then easing his grip a bit.

Hearing the cops rattle the door, probably looking through the showroom window. Remembering what Jackie said about the cops finding something at the car lot. Maybe trying to set Randy up, too. The three of us not moving until the two cops got back in their cruiser and drove off.

Randy still with a grab on my collar, lifting me up, saying, "Dumb fuck, shooting your gun."

"Maybe ask your girlfriend, see who called."

"Saying what, Jackie called?" Shaking his head, tightening his mouth, he swung the tattooed fist, skull and flames and barbed wire with Jackie's name.

I landed in the chair, saw my feet flip up, the chair bucking back. I stayed down, Randy considering his fist, looking at the poster, saying something to Chuvalo I didn't hear.

Taking my cigar box, Pony flipped it open. The two of them helping themselves, puffing a pair of Cubans to life. Tucking away his pistol, Randy told Pony to go ahead. Pony coming around the desk with the drill.

My jaw felt numb, me saying, "I'll get your guns."

Randy putting up a hand, stopping Pony. The two of them talking low, then Randy leaning down, saying, "You got till tomorrow. I got to tell you what happens, you jerk me around, try to split —"

"Yeah, get that reunion with Vick."

"So we understand each other." He told me to show up at the tow yard, gave me till noon, said they'd be watching. The two of them heading out the door, Pony giving me stink eye, not getting to drill my knee. Randy whistling a tune from some TV show, from back when I was a kid, the one with Opie in it. I tried to pull myself up, but then came the blackness.

. . . GETTING IN DEEP

The welt had spread across the side of my face. The puffy eye promised hues of yellow going to eggplant. A spear of pain when I sniffed up blood dripping from my nose. Flecks of it on the Cimarron's seat.

Pulling into the driveway, I knocked over the trash cans, looked around before shutting it off. The hedge had been taken down to stubs. I guessed Tibor got tired of waiting and took his chainsaw to it. Didn't much give a shit about it anymore. Didn't give a shit about the crushed trash can under the front wheel either.

The house sat dark and empty. The door was closed, but it wasn't locked. Going inside, I switched on lights. I lifted the poker from the fireplace, a nice heft to it. Knowing it was going to hurt, I swung it and cleared the Yupik dolls from the mantel, pieces of Yupik flying around the room. Felt good through the pain.

Putting a hand on the wall, I fought the spins, then made it down the hall, switching on more lights, ready to swing the poker at anything coming at me. Rocca's guys, the Bent

Boys, Randy and his assholes, didn't matter. Nobody was putting a hand on me again.

Back in the kitchen, I hit rewind on the answering machine, looking for a box of wine in the pantry, the new messages playing, the first one was Ann's brother-in-law Dennis, saying he'd thought it over, not going to invest, told me he was sorry to hear about Ann leaving, told me not to be a stranger, Debra bitching and Dennis Jr. screaming in the background.

Second message was from Ted. "Jeff, what the hell? Where are you? Call me soon as you get this." Followed by a beep and another message from Ted. "Call me, goddamn it."

I dialed the number, voice mail picking up at the other end. Hanging up, I slid down the wall, dropping the poker next to me.

Maybe a good thing Randy took my Ruger from me. Thinking of Vick talking about the best way to off himself.

The phone rang and I pushed myself up the wall, picked it up and just listened.

"Jeff?" Ted's voice.

"Yeah."

"What the fuck, leave me hanging like that," he said.

"Just got in. Not going to believe —"

"I'm going bat-shit crazy here."

"Hold on, you hear about Vick?"

"Fuck Vick. I need you to get over here, now."

"Forget it."

"You son of a bitch. They just found one of the guns, behind the fucking Coke machine, right in the fucking showroom." Yelling about the cops showing at his place with a search warrant, yelling some more how an Uzi got behind the pop machine.

I tried to tell him what Jackie had said, but he wasn't listening.

"Who's got my Caddy, you or Vick?"

"I'm trying to tell you about Vick —"

"He got it?"

"Vick's gone."

"With the car?"

"He's dead, you asshole."

Silence.

"What?"

Pain forced me to slide back down and sit on the floor. I tried to explain it, what Jackie had told me about Vick. "Cops think he might've offed himself."

"Cops everywhere, Jesus. You talk to them?"

"Not since the showroom got shot up." I thought for a moment. "Maybe too much for him, Vick cranking that heap to life and gassing himself."

"What's wrong with that guy?"

"Well, he's dead, for one."

"Jesus," Ted said, then, "Well, maybe it's best."

"How's dead best?"

"The memos, the hair shows. Elvis fucking Christ. Don't know what he was like on the inside, but on the outside, that guy was . . . All I know, it was him, hiding the fucking gun behind the Coke machine. Just . . . how'd he get it?"

"Know what, Ted, you're all heart. How about you go fuck yourself."

Could hear him puffing, then he said, "Look, okay, I'm sorry the guy's dead, really. Jesus, who needs that. Maybe he wasn't so bad. He leave a memo, a note, something like that?"

"According to Jackie, cops are calling it asphyxiation, for now anyway, all I know."

"Bad timing all the way around. Look, I'm not going to make the funeral. Got to take off, a while anyway. Get Bonnie to send an arrangement, something nice, befitting."

"She quit, remember?"

"Yeah, shit," he said, sounding like he was coming undone. "Everything going to hell. Can't get a hold of Mateo either. He call you?"

"Didn't call, didn't show up. Your man Bucky swung by, told us we were taking the Peace Bridge, said he got the word from Mateo, nobody calling to say different. Made it across —"

"Alright, alright . . ." Ted stopping me, saying Bucky told him the same thing. "Till I know what's what, time to keep a low profile, keep them from slapping on an ankle tether, so, I'm asking again, where's the Caddy?"

"Right in the driveway."

I started to tell him what Jackie said, about planting something at the showroom, I heard banging over the line, sounded like someone was rapping at his door.

Ted saying, "Shit." Sounded like he laid the phone down.

Feeling the walls close in, fighting the pain and dizziness, thinking if Jackie called the cops, they'd be coming around here, too, ex-cons always at the top of the suspect list.

. . . THE THREE COUNT

"Hang on." Setting the phone down, Ted cat-stepped to the door, hoping it was Ginger, the service sending her over early. Checking the peephole, he froze. Three men stood outside, one in a suit, uniformed cops like bookends to either side of him.

The one in the suit knocked again, Ted standing still, his breath catching.

Reaching in his jacket, the middle one took his badge and tapped it against the peephole, saying, "We see your shadow, Mr. Bracey."

If it wasn't Vick, could be Marcel gave him up, maybe Mateo, one of these assholes cutting a deal. Maybe Jeff.

"Go easier if you open it." The one in the suit nodded at the other two. Drawing his sidearm, he took a step back and said, "Gonna count to three . . ."

Ted was backing across the room, no place to run.

"Ted?" Jeff's voice called through the phone. "Ted, Ted."

. . . BETWEEN JOBS AGAIN

Just the photos left on the mantel, the wedding photo of the two of us in better days, fading Kodak color. I set it down, stepped on a bit of Yupik doll, hop-stepped in pain, then took the photo of Ann's family and tossed in the fireplace, the glass cracking. Sinking my weight into the sofa cushion, I stared at the TV that wasn't on, caught my reflection on the screen, imagining my own eulogy: Jeff Nichols — blind-sided by life — never saw it coming.

Seeing the indents on the old rug where Ann's chair had stood, I thought, man, I could use a drink. Reaching the remote, I clicked on a M*A*S*H rerun, Klinger telling Radar how he was getting out. Clicking again, I got Mike Tyson saying no to drugs, then an Uncola commercial.

A sound from out back had me clicking the mute and reaching for the poker. Somebody coming for me, maybe the cops. I edged to the sidelight, peeking out at the night through the pebbled glass. Tibor's ratty dog rummaged around my garbage cans. No lights on next door, no Firebird on my boulevard lawn, just the stumps from the cedar hedge, looked like a line of broken teeth.

Going to the cupboard, I found a box of Ritz and slid off the back door's chain. Fumbling the switch for the back porch light, nothing out there but the dog. Dumping crackers on the stoop, I watched the dog come sniffing and licking, crunching up the crackers, keeping one eye on me. Closing the door, I slid the chain back on, and it hit me.

Why Ted wanted the Cimarron. Randy wanting it, too.

Grabbing the keys and the poker, I went out the front, backed the car off the trash can, then rolled to the garage, switching spots with my old Valiant. With my vision impaired, I scraped the Cimarron, taking off the passenger-side mirror on the doorframe. I rolled it in, Tibor's dog watching me.

Closing the garage door, I jacked up the Caddy's back end, shoved a cinder block under the frame, then cranked up the other side. Grabbing my trouble light, I slid underneath. No sign that Mateo's guys had added cells. Remembering Marcel Banks saying how they opened on hydraulics, the cars rigged so you had to put your foot on the brake and turn the key at the same time, flip a switch under a fake bottom on the console. Sliding from under the chassis, I opened the driver's door and tried the sequence, finding the switch, hearing the clunk of metal from underneath.

. . . HOOPED

The fence boards stood high enough to block the yard from the street. Turning the Cimarron into the gravel lot, I pulled up in front of the craggy office, looked like a construction trailer with the wheels knocked off, faded paint blistering and peeling from the siding. There was the same Harley I'd seen at Vick's, flames painted on its gas tank, leaned on its kickstand, parked next to another bike, this one chopped, painted flat black. Old tires hung from spikes at what looked like an old tool shed, license plates from all over were nailed to the boards like trophies.

The orange tow truck rolled in, hauling a junker Ford into the impound lot, rolling behind the office, stirring up dust. A sign on the door of the trailer: Hooper Towing Yard — Salvage, Recovery and Repo. If your car's out back, you're hooped.

Everyone's a comedian.

Leaving her running, I opened the door, put my leg out. Randy came from the trailer, one of my Cohibas in his mouth, saying it was his last one. Smiling, he took the steps, inspecting the facial he'd given me, looking at his tattooed fist, saying, "Ain't lost my touch."

"Yeah, your mama'd be proud."

"Bent it just like your man Chuvalo's." He pointed at my own nose. "Next guy's liable to think twice before taking a swing."

Looking at the banged-up front end and missing mirror on the Caddy, Randy said, "And somebody kicked the shit out of your ride too, huh?"

"The whackos are out there, let me tell you."

"And seems you got a knack for pissing them off," Randy said, reaching in for a fistful of my shirt.

"I took the guns out." I clutched the wheel.

He looked at me, then let go, saying, "Make it good."

"Got six, but we don't do it here."

"Telling me how it is, huh?"

"Yeah, and they're a grand apiece."

He started smiling, saying, "Really pushing the luck, uh?"

"Earned something. You want 'em or not?"

"Being able to walk's something." He tapped the roof and backed off, said yeah, he was interested.

I caught Pony looking out the office window, picking up a clipboard and looking back at my car.

Randy saying, "What's your plan?"

"Going to the funeral?"

"Yeah, me and the man had some history."

"Bring the cash."

He thought about it, then nodded, and I shut the door and slung an arm over the seat and backed out of there, stirring some dust.

In my rearview I saw Pony step out next to Randy, holding up his clipboard, pointing a finger at it, showing it to Randy. The two of them laughing, looking as I rolled out.

Rhinestone-studded leather, Archie the Elvis walked his Vegas swagger between the rows of plots, glitzing like it was the City of Lights. Hair greased and combed back. His collar up, a string tie around his neck. Snakeskin boots and dark shades. The mother I had seen at Marcel's barbershop had her arm hooked through Ed's, no sign of the kids. Archie looking like he might break out in song, "Don't Cry Daddy" or something fitting the occasion, something Vick would have liked.

The turnout was decent and had me wondering how many would attend my own funeral. Something that could happen, if things didn't work out. No family to speak of, Ann gone from my life now. Vick, too. No brotherhood with any of the guys back in the Don. Just a priest and some guy hired to lean on a shovel. I pictured myself laid out in a box in my ripped suit. Guess it wouldn't much matter if I was dead.

Randy looked over and I nodded. The way Pony had come out of that trailer, pointing to the clipboard. I guessed a repo list was attached, the feds quick to seize anything with Ted Bracey's name attached, the AutoPark and every car on the lot, searching for more guns.

If my plan worked, I'd be blowing town with more money than I'd ever had. Before I headed for the funeral, I wrote a note for Penny Mansell to get the money the broker was holding in trust back to Ann, giving her Debra and Dennis's address in Montreal. I faxed it to her office.

Vick's Auntie Jean had delivered the eulogy back at the Tabernacle of Faith, not a dry eye in the place, the woman reflecting how she raised Vick from a tender age, touching on his life's highlights, saying he was a well-mannered boy, full of hope and joy, getting the grades, volunteering at the pet shelter, played forward for the peewee hockey team, set a goal-scoring record, recounting his Boy Scout badges, how she watched him slug his first homer for the Junior Jays. Now she stood crying, rocking Tina the schnauzer in her arms, the dog with a black ascot instead of a collar.

The two bereaved women standing opposite had to be the ex-wives, one shorter, with child-bearing hips and Latino looks. Both looking good in black. A girl of maybe thirteen stood to the right of the taller one, mirroring her father's features, likely a daughter Vick had never talked about. Ricki stood next to them, looking sad, modestly dressed in black.

Leaning close to Jackie, Randy spoke in hushed tones, the woman nodding, both of them glancing my way.

Accenting a solemn look, the priest came along a path in his white vestments, took his place at the head of the casket, handing Ricki a basket of white carnations, patting her arm, consoling her, one flower intended for each of the mourners to lay on the casket as it was lowered. Clearing his throat to get all heads bowing, he delivered the last rites.

I got flashes of talking to Vick in the yard at the Don,

running into him again at Marcel's, the flight to Poughkeepsie, the hookers that night, the two of us driving back. So many things that could have turned out different. If I had listened to Ann and got myself a nine-to-five, maybe I could have adjusted to suburban life. Maybe Vick would still be alive, spinning his circles and doing cardboard furniture deals, turning film tanks into breeding pools for trout, hiring guys dressed like Elvis and sending his memos. Don't know why, but I started smiling.

Just as quick, I sobered, thinking Ann would meet a new man, a nine-to-fiver. Thoughts of her climbing into a strange bed gave me a shiver, her having some other man's baby. Picturing a birthday cake with a single candle, the nine-to-fiver's mouth helping to blow out the candle. Getting called Daddy. Blinking away tears, I bowed my head, tried clinging to the priest's words, something about rewards in the Hereafter. Souls of the righteous in the hands of God, no torment ever touching them, forever at peace.

Finally, turning my bruised eyes up to the rolling clouds, I spotted the orange tow truck pulling through the cemetery gates about a hundred yards off. First thought, it was Randy's ride home. The guy having no class, going to a funeral with cockeyed Jackie in his orange tow truck. I caught Randy nudging her, the woman grinning my way some more. Something was up.

"And so, let us consider Victor's dash, the line bridging the date of his arrival to the date of departure," the priest went on, saying the dash represented how our dear Victor spent his time on Earth.

The clamor of the tow truck's hydraulic stinger arm

carried past the line of parked cars, heard above the priest's words about a man's wealth, working in the Lord's service, cherishing thy brethren, offering a kindness and a helping hand. The priest asking those gathered to put value in our own dash and to think about that and make the most of our time here on Earth.

The assembled saying, "Amen."

The driver was Pony, working the controls, the stinger arm extending, the wheel cradles sliding in place.

"And so, in closing, dear friends, I invite you to place a flower . . ." The priest calling this a final gesture of love, ending with, "May you rest in peace, dear Victor. Amen."

The mourners turned and started lining at Ricki's basket, each taking one and laying a flower on Vick's casket. Taking my place in line, I looked back at the tow truck. Tossing my flower, I was saying, "So long, Vick."

Working the hydraulics, Pony closed the brackets and cradled the whitewalls. Lifting the tow boom, he raised the front of the car.

Coming up beside me, tossing his flower on the casket, Randy took hold of my arm. "Case you're slow putting things together," Randy said, "I got what I came for." Nodding at the tow truck, the Cimarron in back, saying, "And don't go worrying about a ride, you're coming with me."

"Don't think so."

"You're fucked, either way."

I figured on that part, knowing he wasn't going to pay me, or let me walk away. Soon as he had his guns . . .

"Hey, fuck!" I jerked from his grip

Randy caught off guard as I shot off like a sprinter,

yelling some more, "Nothing's goddamned sacred — hey, hey, you asshole, that's my car!"

Thunderstruck, the priest stumble-stepped and crossed himself. Heads turning my way, Vick's Auntie Jean gasping, the ex-wives clutching each other, Ricki dropping the basket, a hand to her bosom. Randy and Jackie watching me do the potter's-field sprint, dodging between headstones, jumping a plaque.

Tearing across the grounds, adrenaline coursing my veins, I wove in and out, leaping another plaque, doing it in spite of the pain in my body. The soft earth of a newly turned grave tugged off my shoe. Stumbling on, I caught my balance on a stone and kept going.

It must've been the last straw for Tina, I didn't know it then, the schnauzer springing free from Auntie Jean's embrace and racing after me.

Running on, I startled a kneeling couple clearing weeds and replacing flowers for beloved Mother, paying their respects.

"Hey, cocksucker, yeah, you!" I yelled it, a stitch ripped at my side like an ice pick, God's vengeance, me having a meltdown in this place of rest. It slowed me, but I kept on.

Looking over as I ran at him, Pony appeared surprised, then he grinned, his look saying he could swat me like a bug. Maybe he figured he got what he was after, thinking the guns were on board the Caddy, and I'd been beaten down as much as any man needed to be. Swinging into the driver's seat, he slapped the door shut and put her in gear, smiling like he was doing me a favor. Rolling out with the Cimarron in tow.

Catching myself on a headstone, I gasped down air, watching the tow truck roll through the cemetery gates. Not wanting to be anywhere near these guys when they found out the guns weren't there.

Being out of shape had me buckling over and vomiting on the words *In loving memory*. The other thing I hadn't counted on cleared the last row of headstones, Tina bearing down, snarling and leaping past the last plot. Bent over, I turned just as she jumped like a dog on a guy-wire, her jaws open and snapping. Man, those schnauzers can bite.

. . . CANARIES

"Where'd you park?" Conway Forbes swung back his front door, cue-ball head looking polished. Crimson bathrobe half open, a medallion on a chain hanging down, white socks inside sandals, a defiance to anybody's fashion sense.

I pointed to my old Valiant between two land boats across the street, the back seat and trunk crammed with everything I owned, three Uzis in the trunk, as many under the junk on the back seat.

After the cemetery, I'd flagged a cab to where I'd parked the Valiant at a mall near the house and called Randy from a pay phone, asked how the hell he was doing, told him what he figured was in the Caddy was going to cost him fifteen hundred a piece now, plus ten for the cab ride. I gave him the number of the pay phone, was telling him I'd give him ten minutes to decide. He told me to get fucked, and I said it was worth a shot, that I'd call the Bent Boys, see how much they'd give me, then I hung up. The phone rang in seconds, Randy saying fine, fifteen hundred. I named a spot up past Kleinburg, told him to leave his psycho friends at home, knowing he wouldn't, then hung up. Taking out the piece of paper, the number Ted had given me for Jerrel Bent's guys, the two guys in the black Suburban.

The way I timed it, I guessed I had time to stop in here, at Conway's, en route. Don't know why, but somehow I figured I was paying respect to Vick.

Looking out at the Valiant, I said to Conway, "Yeah, the old girl's been leaking oil. Didn't want to get any on your driveway."

Thanking me, Conway asked me to take off my shoes on account of his new wall-to-wall, then he ushered me in, saying, "Guess you two met, huh?"

Robbie Boyd stuck his head around the corner of the hall, his hand still taped up. Smiling, he offered me his good hand, telling Conway I was the one who asked him to pop over.

"Tough racket, huh, the car biz?" Conway said, looking from Robbie's bandaged hand to my bruised face.

"You got no idea," I said, limping into his converted living room, "but all that's in the rearview now." When I grinned I felt my lip split again, mopping my tongue over it. Pulling out the wrinkled pamphlet, I said, "Vick was going on how you got people singing. And I knew Robbie was looking for something new. Vick calling this man a marketing whiz." If Jackie Delano could get away with it, why not Robbie.

Robbie tried not looking surprised, Conway looking at him appraising.

"Guess it was Vick's last big idea, bringing Robbie in as a kind of marketing whiz."

"That Vick had a nose for this stuff, uh?" Conway said.

"Sure did."

Robbie and I smiling at each other.

Conway smiled, too, holding his hand up Vanna White–style — same way Ann used to — showing us the front room converted into a sound studio, the place where he recorded and taught anyone to sing like a canary. Pointing out the mixing desk, an impossible tangle of cords out the back, Conway saying, "Got forty channels, three thousand watts and a thirty-band equalizer."

Setting a hand on the Baldwin, I eased weight off my chewed leg, Robbie putting his back against the wall. Conway showing off the line of electrics hanging from pegs: Les Paul, Strat, Tele, a twelve-string Rickenbacker. I nodded. At another time I would have been thinking how much I could hawk this stuff for.

Conway went on about a Flying V up in the bedroom, and a Gretsch like Chet played, case anybody wanted to see more, asking, "Either of you boys shred?"

Robbie held up the hand with the missing finger, and I told Conway no, taking in the rest of the room. Looked like egg cartons nailed on the walls and ceiling. A PA system, a bunch of speakers, a Twin Reverb, a Mesa Boogie, a tube Marshall.

Conway told us about meeting Vick at the trade show, asked if we heard about his cardboard chairs, retelling how he sold out at the Five Man Electrical Band show. I grinned at Robbie, didn't say Vick made the real money from the fire he set afterwards.

"May God rest his soul," Conway said, looking down at his white socks in sandals, crossing himself and adding the man had been plucked in his prime.

Robbie and I saying, "Amen."

"Shame he didn't see the hair thing through," Conway said. "Know it's going to be big."

"Amen to big," Robbie said. "That's Vick for you, a man ahead of his time."

"A head of his time, I like that," Conway said, nodding at Robbie like he was impressed. "A head of his time." Thanking me for setting this up, he said Robbie might just be the man he needed. Clapping his hands, saying, "What say I show you gents my stuff?" He put an arm around Robbie. "Let's give it a try."

"All you'll get from me's croaking," Robbie said, "marketing's more my thing."

Conway wasn't listening, saying, "First we loosen the pipes."

"My folks used to coax me," I said. "Got me singing when I was a kid, mostly for company. Everybody standing around the booze cabinet, one with the console stereo, speakers on the sides, turntable on top. Put me front and center. Guess I was the source of amusement at martini hour, around the time of Lawrence Welk and that Mitch guy with the bouncing balls. Drunken relatives laughing and going, 'Hey, Artie, ease up on the olives, and by the way, your kid sings like crap.' Guess that stuff struck a nerve, stayed with me." Not sure why I told them.

"We can fix that," Conway said. "Fact, anyone can breathe, can sing."

Robbie wiped his wrapped hand at his eyes, and I knew it was time to go.

Conway was all the way into it now, saying, "We all possess the urge to sing, brother, a primal thing that frees the soul." Bending from the waist, scratching inside his white sock, he said he practically guaranteed it, telling Robbie he'd have him singing in no time, but in time. Then he sang the scales, raising the flat of his hand from low to high, holding each note for a couple of measures, urging Robbie to give it a try.

Hesitating, Robbie gave it a shot, missing every note.

Conway put a hand on Robbie's forehead, his fingers splayed spider-like, saying to him, "Just a bit flat on your la las."

Checking the Timex again, I edged for the door, putting my shoes on. "Well, fellas, best of luck. Glad it's working out. Do it for Vick, huh?"

Telling me to hold on, Conway rushed to a rack and took a cassette and handed it to me, saying, "Sing with me, brother, anytime you want. And thank you for hooking us up, and do call, you change your mind, can join the team anytime you want."

Thanking him, I said I was heading out of town and wouldn't be back, nodding to Robbie, wishing him luck.

Conrad was back beside him, slinging an arm around Robbie like he might bolt for the door, saying, "How about we try some Burt." And before Robbie could answer, Conway said, "And don't be afraid to set it to dance." Singing a line about what you get when you fall in love, he did a ballet leap that landed him in front of the Baldwin, saying to me as I did up the laces, "Got some folks coming by, booked the studio for a tribute to Bhaktivedanta Swami Prabhupada. Hope to have Robbie singing along."

"Bet you will," I said, standing and giving a final nod to

Robbie. Turning for the door, I saw figures moving through the ribbed sidelight, coming up the walk. Swallowed the panic. Patted the pocket for the piece that was out under the seat of the Valiant. All the guns out there.

Conway saying as the doorbell chimed, "Should be here any — ahh." Then he angled past me and swung back the door, saying, "Hari hari." Ushering in a half dozen Hare Krishnas, white noses, shaved heads with sikhas, wearing saffron dhotis and saris, some holding instruments: mridangas, karatalas and tambourines. Squeezing past the second coming — the Age of Aquarius — I crossed the street to the Valiant, getting in and hoping she'd fire up, boxes and bags of my belongings stuffed in the back.

Cranking the ignition, I coaxed her to life and drove on. Finding a strip mall with a pay phone next to a place called the Donut Hole, the smell of pastry wafting from the place getting me hungry. The smell from the laundromat next door bringing my stomach back to Earth. Looking around, I dug a quarter from my pocket, found the piece of paper with the number Ted had given me and made the call. Maybe the last one I'd ever make. Pretty sure it was the one called Blue Eyes who answered, and I said, "Got a delivery from Ted."

It took a second, then he said, "Say again?"

I repeated it, then he said, "You the one with the crazy neighbor, uh?"

"Yeah, the guy's Russian, just like the stuff from Ted, it's Russian, too. You want them or not?"

"How many we talking?"

"Six."

"If you screwing with me —"

I told him when and where and how much, then I asked if he wanted more than just the six.

"Hell yeah."

"Bring five more Gs, and I'll point you right to it." And before he could say anything else, I told him he had a half hour, and I hung up.

. . . THE PROMISED LAND

The spongy feel of the brakes and the cough coming from the pipe had me thinking I'd be jacking a fresh ride before I got anywhere near the Big Nickel — if I lived that long. Jacking rides, right back to it, maybe the only thing I was ever any good at. But I wasn't going back to it, that or any of the old ways that never panned out. This was me starting over, going for broke and moving forward.

Passing through Rexdale, I slid Conway's cassette in the player, the man singing the same Bacharach number. Humming along as I neared Kleinburg. Doing it to keep me calm, I started singing along, the words to the song I remembered.

The single headlight in the rearview reminded me again of the old Sing Along with Mitch show. Back when I was a kid with only a handful of channels on the round dial. The bouncing ball turned into a second, then a third. I was singing along, faking half the words.

Bada da da bada da da — kissing girls — bad da and getting pneumonia.

The bouncing balls were headlights, getting bigger in the rearview. I let them come, the sound of the motorcycles rising over the two of us singing — never falling in love again.

. . . BLOWING OUT

The old car blew foul exhaust through Kleinburg. Checking my watch, I tried to remember these roads — my life depending on it — hanging a right as the Harleys gained. Randy Hooper on the vintage FXR, switching to the passing lane and pulling alongside, motioning for me to pull over.

Rolling down my window, I pointed up ahead.

He went to pass, and I swerved to keep him back. The smack of metal on metal. Pony was swinging a bike chain at my rear bumper, trying to wrap it and rope the Valiant like a steer. Swerving into the oncoming lane, I shot up on the next county road, feeling the thunk of the chain on the bumper.

Going wide to the opposite shoulder, Randy easily blew past me. Luther rolling up on my passenger side, the three of them boxing me in. Just a little more time. Cranking the wheel, I let Luther know I wasn't playing. If they wanted the Uzis, they'd have to get dirty.

A pistol showed in Randy's tattooed hand, the man trying to get a bead. Luther was kicking at my passenger door, his bike swerving in and out, and Pony kept swinging the chain, getting it wrapped around the bumper. Nobody else on the side road.

Trying to push away the feeling of doom.

Grinning in the passenger window, Luther laid a boot at the door. Cranking a hard right, I forced him onto the gravel shoulder, the man fighting for control, cursing and leveling a gonna-kill-your-ass look.

Turning on his seat, Randy put a round through the rad, and I mashed my gas pedal, not enough power to ram him. The whole box was rattling.

A yellow sign marked the curve ahead, King Vaughan coming up. I gripped the wheel in both hands.

Twisted on his seat, Randy fired again, the windshield bursting in, Luther was kicking, and Pony was yanking. Nothing to do but hold on and steer. Conway Forbes still singing on the tape deck.

Catching the glimmer in the rearview as we hit the curve, sure it was the black Suburban, I yelled out and ripped the parking brake up from the floor, the ass end of the Valiant sweeping around, another window smashing. Shoving the handle down, I slammed on the gas, sideswiping Randy, sending the Harley into the oncoming lane. Losing control, he dumped the bike.

Hammering the brakes, I felt Pony smack into the rear end, losing sight of him as he went down. The Valiant slid on the gravel, forcing Luther's bike into the ditch on the right. Pony went tumbling past, his bike cartwheeling in the lane, then flipping end over end and bounding over the fence rail and into the field on the opposite side.

Sending up a cloud of dust, I plowed nose first into the

bank, thrown into the steering wheel, my head smacking the windshield.

Half blind, I grabbed for an Uzi on the back seat, under the junk that had slid around. Shouldering open the door, I scrambling out, smelling spilled fuel. I hobbled around the back, seeing Pony's bloody finger attached to the chain wrapped around my bumper. Luther was getting to his feet behind me, blood matting his hair, drawing his pistol.

I tried to make a grove of trees, a horse trailer parked past a gate, the black earth of a field that had been plowed over. Fire flicked from under the Valiant's crumpled hood.

The stabbing pain had me thinking I'd been shot. Going for the gate, I did a half turn, saw Pony laid out like a speed bump on the tarmac, his arms and legs splayed. Same time the Suburban rounded the bend, coming too fast to do anything but vault over him, the undercarriage snagging leather and dragging the man. Rear wheels hopping and spitting Pony out the back. Losing control, the big Chevy was swept off the road, slamming the back of the Valiant, the Bent Boys bouncing around inside.

Ducking behind an oak, I checked the Uzi, the clip empty. Randy White rose up and tossed away his lid and crossed the lane, bending for Pony's pistol. Luther forgetting about me and going down the passenger side of the Suburban. The windows rolled down and gun barrels were shoved out. Randy put a round through the driver's side, likely killing Dirty Leg. He kept on shooting. Luther firing from the other side. Jerrel and Blue Eyes spilled out the passenger side, both rolling into the ditch, returning fire. Everybody shooting. Conway singing from the shot-out windows of the burning Valiant, the flames spreading through the interior.

The shooting stopped, and Randy stood over Jerrel Bent, both of them bleeding, pointing pistols at each other. Both men saying something, both looking toward me, then firing at each other, point blank. Randy staggered back and fired again, making sure. Then he looked my way.

Conway singing about Love Sweet Love. I lifted the Uzi, holding it up.

Reaching in his pocket, Randy pulled out the stub of a Cuban, stuck it in his mouth, flicked a lighter and dragged on it, then he sank to his knees and slumped to the ground. Nobody else moving. Smoke rose from under the Valiant's hood, flames licking up the interior, still Conway was singing.

I walked past who I took for Jerrel Bent, stopped by Blue Eyes and bent over him. A surprised look on his face and his mouth open. His pockets gave up a wad of cash, money for the guns. The extra five grand, too. Shoving it in my pocket, I said, "No need to count it, I trust you fellas." I dropped the Uzi next to him, said the rest were in there, pointing to the burning car. A deal's a deal.

The tape was heating, Conway's voice sounding wonky, singing about a great big freeway.

The stabbing in my side kept up as I walked to the Suburban, opening the driver's door, easing Dirty Leg out and laying him in the road. The keys were in the ignition, the tank gauge read full.

I backed from the flaming wreck and pulled past it, the cassette and tape deck starting to melt. Conway's singing becoming distorted, something about stars that never were and asking if I knew the way to someplace. I pulled away, the Valiant's tank catching and the whole mess blowing up.

Driving along that back road, thinking that didn't work out too bad. Thinking I'd head north till I hit the next town, find someplace to eat, knowing I'd need to start thinking about jacking a fresh ride. The cops would be looking for this one. Maybe looking for me, too. I took out the roll of bills, and with one eye on the road, I counted out my fresh start.

ACKNOWLEDGMENTS

As always, a big thank you goes to Jack David for his ongoing support. And to the great people at ECW who get it right and make it fun. It's a pleasure to work with them. Many thanks to my brilliant editor, Emily Schultz. And for the keen eye of copy editor Peter Norman who catches everything, and David Gee who perfectly conveys the essence of my stories with his cover designs. Also to my son, Xander, for allowing me to bounce story ideas off him, and for tolerating my silly notions and mischief.

And, of course, to Andie.